A Dream Called Marilyn

MERCEDES KING

BOOKS BY MERCEDES KING

The Jacqueline Bouvier Kennedy Onassis Collection

Jackie's Paris

Jackie's Camelot

Jackie's Greece

Jackie's New York

Historical Fiction Titles

A Dream Called Marilyn

Crime Fiction / Mysteries

Every Little Secret

Grave Secrets

Columbus Noir

Newsletter subscribers receive a FREE e-book for joining. Sign-up here.

PROLOGUE

Charles paused on the sidewalk, his attention suddenly captured by the flash of her picture on a digital billboard. He missed it earlier, on his way into the doctor's office, but now a near-paralysis rooted him to the concrete as he stared upward.

"What is it, Grandpa?" His grandson touched his arm.

With the summer breeze fluffing the tufts of his white hair, Charles couldn't take his eyes off the billboard. He waited for her picture to reappear. Of course, it wasn't *her*, but an ad touting a female impersonator who would be performing nightly at the local casino.

Still, long buried memories began to surface. Charles bent as his knees grew shaky, and his chest tightened.

"Are you okay, Grandpa?" The young man helped Charles to a nearby bench shaded by a tree.

Catching his breath, Charles glanced up again at the phony persona.

Had he been a better man, he knew her life would've turned out differently. Whatever he had done right by the actress paled compared to how he failed her. Deserted her, really, when she was most vulnerable. With only himself to blame. Even now, decades later, he couldn't rationalize what had happened during those summer days in June of

1962. Weeks later, when he heard the news of her death—by *suicide*—guilt harnessed him, like a ball and chain he couldn't detach.

He looked at his beloved, twenty-something year-old grandson with dull gray eyes. Pride and envy swelled within Charles, knowing the young man, ripe with athleticism and vigor, like Charles at that age, had his whole life ahead of him. A clean slate to fill with adventures and mistakes.

"I knew her once."

"Who?" asked the young man.

"Marilyn Monroe." Charles pointed toward the billboard.

The young man laughed, but when he checked his grandfather's deadpan expression, any hint of humor seemed to leave him. Charles assumed the boy suddenly believed him and was now intrigued.

"When?"

Charles hesitated and looked away. Was now the time to delve into his brief relationship with the icon? Should he tamper with the perceptions the boy held of the legendary sexpot and expose the kind of man Charles had been back then?

His time with Marilyn was complicated and rife with secrets. Not just Marilyn's secrets, but revelations that would up-end his family's history and would redefine what his grandson knew to be true.

"Maybe I shouldn't." Regret began to creep over Charles.

"It's okay, Grandpa. You can tell me anything."

No good reason existed for Charles to unearth his past. There was no chance for justice to prevail. No chance of redemption for himself —or Marilyn. But when Charles glimpsed his grandson's now-eager expression, he knew it was too late to backpedal. Capping the subject wouldn't be an option.

Maybe it's finally time, Charles thought. *Time someone else knew the whole truth, and for me to own my mistakes.*

Of course, he hadn't processed the news he just received from his doctor, but did it matter?

"You're not likely to believe much of this." Charles swallowed but failed to suppress the lump in his throat. "Who knows how this will all sound, coming from an old man, but Marilyn Monroe almost ran away with me."

ONE

Dr. Charles Campbell tightened the knot in his tie, knowing that today was the biggest day of his career. Maybe even his life. He promised himself that he wouldn't let his infatuation get the best of him. That when she walked into his office and they met for the very first time, he wouldn't become a caricature, dumfounded by her beauty and stardom.

He'd spent the morning cleaning the space. Wiping away dust and eliminating clutter. Making sure his diplomas hung T-square straight and his hands were washed thoroughly. His gray suit and navy-blue tie were pressed to perfection.

Like most red-blooded males he took a beating from inside his chest whenever he saw her on the screen. Not that he'd seen all of her movies, but Charles knew she had a way about her. With that teasing smile and naivety she exuded, combined with her voluptuous figure, she stirred a man's desires effortlessly. Charles dabbed away the beads of perspiration from his forehead and blinked hard to stop the rushing images in his head. Today required focus.

After all, his services were needed. An executive from Twentieth Century Fox had visited his Los Angeles office last week and asked if he'd be interested in taking on a *special* case. A distressed actress.

Discretion was a must. So was urgency. Intrigued, Charles agreed. The studio contact left him a file detailing the woman's medical history and scheduled her appointment. Peeking through the pages after the man left, Charles finally discovered who he'd be treating—Marilyn Monroe. The demands for discretion and urgency became apparent.

Now, anticipating her arrival, he shored up his resolve. She wasn't the first celebrity in desperate need of a psychiatrist, and she wouldn't be the first to cross his office threshold. A variety of actors had been in his care. Those struggling with sexual identity issues, depression, anger, insomnia, alcohol...the list went on.

He straightened the magazines atop the coffee table again to occupy himself. Glancing around the outer office, he wondered what she would notice. The paintings or furnishings? Or would she happen to see Charles' resemblance to Rod Taylor? Maybe she'd remark that his hair was lighter, but the similarities were uncanny. He'd heard it plenty of times. Perhaps his only hope was that she

A knock sounded, interrupting his rambling thoughts.

Charles opened the door to his office.

And there she was.

"Miss Monroe." He stepped aside and held out his hand to welcome her in. "Please."

She smiled warmly. Charles detected a hint of apprehension in her gorgeous eyes as she entered. A crème-colored sheath dress covered her curves while a matching shawl draped her shoulders. Interesting, Charles thought, for a sultry June afternoon.

"It's a pleasure to meet you, Miss Monroe." Charles offered his hand.

Marilyn stole a surmising glance of the outer office, which served as the waiting area for Charles' practice. She shook his hand and paired it with a mild shoulder shrug.

"Thank you for seeing me, Dr....?"

Charles reddened. "Dr. Campbell." Hadn't the studio contact mentioned his name to her? And as the man from the studio crossed his mind, he found it curious Marilyn had come alone. Since he gave the impression Marilyn was unbalanced and the mattered needed handled carefully, Charles expected her to be escorted. "May I get you anything? A glass of water perhaps?"

"No, thank you." She smiled, sweetly yet cautiously. Charles couldn't blame her. Here was a woman who'd been raised in turmoil, endured multiple heartbreaks and divorce, along with professional difficulties. Much of it in the public eye while being rotated through various doctors and prescriptions.

"Would you like to sit here or in the other room?" He indicated the inner office, its door ajar. "There's a couch." Regretting his word choices, heat blazed over him. "I only mention it because it may be more comfortable." He snapped his mouth shut, worried he sounded unintentionally lewd and unprofessional.

"Wherever you'd like me."

The lump that jumped into his throat almost knocked him unconscious. He slipped his forefinger behind his shirt collar and slid it along his neckline. Minutes into his first session and he was blowing it! Did he have any hope left of instilling confidence in her or in gaining her trust?

To his surprise she laughed. An unexpected, breathy release that made his own breathing pause. She sashayed into the inner office and seated herself on the burnt-orange couch. The sight of her there, with her legs tucked up as she leaned against the armrest, was striking.

He nudged his tie loose and undid the top button of his collar, then followed her in. Was there a sliver of a chance she didn't notice his acute failure to behave better than an ordinary man?

"I know why I'm here." She spoke with a sudden perkiness that caught Charles off guard. Many of his clients had battled resentment and denial while sitting on that couch.

"Yes, we should discuss any issues you're dealing with and concerns you may have." He sat in a tufted vinyl chair across from her. Hope flickered within as his counseling instincts began to take over.

"It's really very simple." Her eyes were wide. Trusting. "You see, I'm dangerous."

"To yourself?"

"Not exactly." A bashful expression swept over her face. "I know it will be hard for you to understand, and I'm not sure how much I should tell you, for your own good."

The disadvantage of only knowing Marilyn for minutes stifled him. He couldn't gauge how serious she was. Still flush from the missteps of their initial encounter, he also needed to declutter his mind from the characters she'd played and the magazine articles he'd skimmed about her. Now was the time to abandon tabloid fodder and discover the real Marilyn.

"Let's be clear now, Miss Monroe." His thoughts flashed to her file and the documented suicide attempts. "Do you think about hurting yourself? Or are you tempted to take too many pills—"

"Why, no, of course not, doctor!"

He let a pause linger, concerned that she became defensive.

"That's good." After a few reassuring nods, he added, "Please, I want you to feel at ease while you're here. It's my intention to provide a comfortable setting, so you can feel safe and free to be candid. That's the best way for us to chart a course of treatment and ensure your good health. Remember, our sessions are completely confidential. Nothing will be shared outside this office."

"You are very kind." Another giggle. "I don't think anyone has cared about keeping me in good health."

Charles didn't know what to say.

"I figured they already told you about me, that I'm dangerous I mean. Isn't that why you agreed to see me so soon?"

"Well, yes, I was immediately concerned for you, but I admit, I know more about your medical history than your current state. Would you mind sharing what you mean by dangerous?"

"You see, Dr. Charlie—Oh! May I call you Dr. Charlie?"

"Certainly," he said slowly, through gritted teeth. Heat spiked around his neck again and pounded into his face. The nickname, and her asking, struck him as condescending.

She seemed pleased, though and said, "Maybe we should talk about you for a moment. I should know a little bit about the man I'm telling all my secrets to."

Irritation poked him. How would he get anywhere with this woman if he couldn't control the conversation? Still, he understood her switching the tables. To build rapport, he'd allow it.

"There isn't much to tell." Charles sighed. "I grew up in New Jersey. Came out here to go to college, Berkley. Opened up my practice and never looked back. Can't say I miss those New Jersey winters."

"But what about your family?" Marilyn planted her chin in her palm and appeared piqued with interest.

"They're still out there. We visit from time to time. It's not easy though, with the distance."

"And you never married?"

Charles caught her glimpsing his bare ring finger. Did he detect a faint blush on his new client?

"Well, I did marry. But...."

"You don't have to tell me." Her shawl slipped when she shrugged, revealing a bare arm. "I know what it's like, ending up in a relationship that isn't what you thought it would be. Even when you love them with everything you've got. One day, you find out that's not good enough— that you're not good enough. That you're a disappointment."

From what Charles knew, she could've been referencing any of her ex-husbands and the difficult turn each of her three marriages had taken. Considering her divorce from playwright Arthur Miller was the most recent, Charles assumed that hurt presently resonated the strongest. Love had been anything but kind—or lasting—for Marilyn. Charles noted the broken heartedness that settled in her eyes. Never had a woman been more attractive to him in that moment. He shook the thought away. Refocused.

"Any children?" Marilyn asked after a beat.

"Two girls."

"You're a very lucky man, then."

He felt a tightening in his chest, knowing that motherhood was an in-bred desire for every woman. But for Marilyn, two miscarriages and an ectopic pregnancy could be added to her lengthy list of losses.

"I'm not a world-famous movie star," Charles said. "You're adored by millions of fans. Why, you're in magazines, and everyone loves your pictures." Usually, Charles detested flattery as an occupational tactic, but he didn't want Marilyn growing despondent after one session. Plus, he had to gauge the level of her ego, as he did with every celebrity client.

"Sometimes I wonder what it would be like, if I'd kept working at the munitions factory and never taken that modeling contract...."

"If you'd be happy?"

"Normal. I'd settle for normal. Maybe happy would follow." She stood and went to the window, abandoning her shawl on the couch. A view of Zettler's Hardware store and the parking lot across the street awaited. "But I know I was meant to be an actress. Sometimes, I just wish it was easier."

"Filmmaking requires long hours, from what I understand."

"And they own you, like a dog with papers or something."

"It angers you?"

She kept her focus on the view. "A little, but you can't fight it. Not really. The movie business is a harsh master. You do what they tell you. Contracts are like dictators! But I'm always hopeful the next film will be different."

Charles considered joining her at the window but held back. He wanted her to have the space she needed, even though the vista was lackluster at best.

"How are you sleeping?" he asked.

She glanced at him over her shoulder, as if she liked the question. "Wonderful."

Although he couldn't identify why, Charles didn't believe her. As with any client, he needed more time to get to know her moods and understand her thinking. With Marilyn, an extra challenge existed, thanks to her skill set as an actress. Charles would have to discern when she was acting and when she was being honest. Equally important to harvest would be the reason why she might mislead him.

"I think I prefer having the whole bed to myself now." Marilyn shifted her attention to Charles' desk. She stepped behind it and ran her fingertips across the desktop. "What's it like being a doctor?"

Before Charles could field an answer, she sat in his chair.

"It must be amazing, to help all those people, to have all the answers." Her ramrod posture seemed even more pronounced. Afternoon sunlight radiated through the window and enhanced her resplendence. "I suppose it's the same as having special powers, like Superman."

"Well, I'm not sure that's a worthy analogy, but thank you. It is important for clients to have faith in you. And to trust you." He bottled the discontent simmering his insides. Never had a client displayed such a lack of boundaries, moving about his office, touching everything.

"I'm sure you're the best in Los Angeles, or else I wouldn't be here. Ralph takes good care of me, but they wanted me to try something different."

And by *they*, Charles assumed she meant the studio executive, Bill Stewart. The man who arranged today's meeting. Evasive with a straight-forward mention of Marilyn's name, he made one point clear: *We need her under control, no matter what it takes.*

Dr. Ralph Greenson, on the other hand, had been one of Marilyn's doctors for a few years and was occasionally featured in the press. According to Bill, *She's been seeing a psychiatrist for years, but we've told her to cut ties. It's time for someone new. More capable of handling her.* Charles wondered if it was because Greenson seemed to be using his association with Marilyn to enrich his own celebrity status rather than to treat her condition.

"Marilyn, I need to ask you, what medications are you taking?"

"I'm not really sure. I take what they tell me." She shrugged. "And sometimes I don't take anything."

And sometimes, Charles thought, *you've taken too much.* Her file provided bare bones about the suicide attempts, which concerned him. According to the reports, she'd overdosed on sleeping pills and barbiturates. He had no idea, though, how in-depth her therapy had been afterwards, but assumed it had not benefitted her much.

Charles needed to do his research and examine the circumstances surrounding each attempt. He wanted to discover what variables contributed to her downfall into depression.

"Why don't you bring in the bottles with you next time. The labels will tell me what I need. Until then, I don't want to give you anything new."

"Mhmm."

He sensed she wasn't listening. The items on his desk now held her interest. Pens, paper, receipt booklet, a clock, telephone. Should he sit there while she rummaged through the drawers next?

"May I have one of these?" She held up a business card she'd taken from the card display on the corner of his desk.

Why, so you can call up Greenson and have a good laugh about me later, since you probably won't remember my name?

"Of course."

"Thank you." She popped up from Charles' chair and came around the side of the desk. "It's been wonderful meeting you." She offered her hand. Charles took it as he stood. "I really think you'll be good for me, doctor. You're very easy to talk to, and I think I like you already."

"Our session isn't over yet, Miss Monroe. We've hardly discussed anything about you."

Before he finished speaking, Marilyn snatched her shawl from the couch, then pecked his cheek with a kiss. A whiff of Chanel perfume danced into his nostrils and made him recall one of her famous quips: What do you wear to bed, Marilyn? She'd replied with: Chanel Number 5.

She was already leaving and called over her shoulder, "That's what tomorrow is for."

ANGER AND EMBARRASSMENT stewed within him, along with a rising desire to ax the arrangement. Who did the woman think she was? Calling him by his first name, sitting at his desk and railroading the entire appointment. Marilyn Monroe was no Elizabeth Taylor, or Grace Kelly for that matter! If their next meeting got out of hand, maybe he'd point that out to *Ms. Monroe*.

Charles slumped into his desk chair. Her vibrant presence lingered, and his agitation began to subside. Truthfully, when was the last time he'd experienced the rocket-fire of emotion she brought? When had exhilaration been so tangible?

Marilyn said she wanted to be normal. Charles laughed to himself. Such a woman had no hope of being *normal*. Or boring. She was luminous, electrifying, and infuriating all at the same time. No wonder several directors and co-stars had complained about working with her.

He had to get past the fireworks of her persona and find a way to rein her in. That was, if he continued seeing her.

———

HIS LAST APPOINTMENT for the day couldn't end soon enough. He scribbled notes into files and ignored the ache in his head. A side effect. Not a result from the last three clients, but from a growing anxiousness to sit back and revisit, in his mind, his time with Marilyn. To replay her every word. Reimagine every gesture.

He couldn't stay angry with her, especially when he recalled her on his couch. She looked relaxed even happy to be there with him. The details of her threatened to consume him. Her smooth legs and unintentional pose. Red-delicious lipstick slicking her pouty lips.

His mind strayed to the scene from *The Seven Year Itch* and her billowing skirt as she strolled over the subway grate. Flirty and playful seemed to be her natural qualities. Or perhaps it was her most comfortable role to play. He wanted to find out and get to know her on a deep, personal level.

Harboring frustrations, he decided, was pointless. Though their time together was brief and punctuated with her unconventional behavior, what did he have to complain about? Marilyn Monroe had been in his office—and they had been alone. Plus, he committed his own infraction—

A knock on his office door interrupted his thoughts. Before Charles could move to answer it, Bill Stewart entered.

"Mr. Stewart, I wasn't expecting to see you today." Charles glanced at his watch, surprised to find it was already after six.

"Glad I caught you." He removed his fedora. "I was in the area, on my way home. Thought I'd drop by and see how your meeting went today."

With a hard-set face that reminded Charles of James Cagney, Bill conveyed arrogance, like most of the studio types Charles had met. Bill cut a sharp figure in his tailored navy suit and projected a no-

nonsense personality. Charles hadn't decided yet how much he liked the man.

"Quite frankly," Charles said, "I thought you'd be with her this afternoon."

Bill seemed to consider that. "Nah. She's a nervous girl at times, but when I told her I set this up, she wanted to come alone. I figured that was best, long as she showed up. She's as unpredictable as she is unstable, if you catch my drift."

Charles disagreed about her instability. Marilyn's attention span was erratic, some of her behavior childlike, but she was more than aware of her allure and the energy of her presence. Bill's comment reminded Charles how people often thought they were able to diagnose others.

"Did you read the file I gave you?" Bill helped himself to a chair and lit a cigarette.

"Yes." Charles joined him in a smoke. "She's been through a lot."

Bill nodded. "Life's no fairy tale for Hollywood's darlings."

"What exactly do you think I can do for her?"

"Can I speak openly here?"

"Certainly."

"Marilyn is a liability for Fox. We've shut down production on her latest project because she was fired from the film."

"Oh?"

"Just recently. She's always late, that is, when she does show, and once she's on set, she spends hours in her dressing room with that wacky acting coach of hers. Filming started months ago, but there's only about ten minutes of usable footage with Marilyn." With his cigarette between his first two fingers, Bill pointed at Charles. "That should give you an idea on the kind of crazy we're dealing with."

"Patients don't like the word crazy."

"Yeah, well, producers don't like losing money. Do you know what a bind this puts us in, a picture with no lead actress? And Marilyn's not a sure thing when it comes to her movies. They don't always make the profit producer want to see. So we want to get this contract fulfilled and move on."

"It's all about money then?"

Bill took a long drag, then exhaled slowly. "In this business, everything's about money, doc."

"She's not a commodity to me." Charles served a mild bite in his tone.

Bill flashed a half-grin. "An hour alone with the girl and you're smitten. Typical."

Charles resented the implication, even though it contained a bit of truth.

"Don't go falling in love, doc, she's not that kind of girl."

"Not to be rude, but you're making too many assumptions, Mr. Stewart. If Marilyn is as fragile and unpredictable as you say, then it's my job to look out for her and find out what's caused her problems. Medications don't treat the root of issues."

Bill enjoyed a chuckle.

"Sure, doc." He reached inside his expensive jacket and withdrew an envelope, then tossed it onto the desktop. "For services rendered this week."

Charles noted the thickness of the envelope.

"Listen, doc, I'm not here to tell you how to do your job." Bill stamped out his cigarette in an ashtray. "But I have to make sure you're doing your job. There are people who want the girl settled and demonstrating a little more self-control."

"You mean medicated but able to work. Hasn't panned out for her so far. And shouldn't you be talking to Greenson about that? He's at fault here, don't you think? Carelessly giving her pills with no concern that she's taking too many."

"I told you, we're not working with Greenson. Forget about him. Right now, she's my top priority—and I need for her to be your top priority. You get me, doc?"

Charles didn't respond with anything more than a steady glare.

"Don't worry, no one's expecting much after one day. For now, we're all good here." He stood and buttoned his jacket as he headed for the door. "I'll be checking in." With his hand on the doorknob, he gave Charles a mischievous glance with a flash of distrust laced in. "Keep your wits about you and don't be fooled. The gal's an actress. She'll lie and use that body to get what she wants, so whatever you do, don't let Marilyn Monroe get under your skin."

As Bill took his leave, Charles began to consider how he would edit and withhold information going forward. Reminding Bill about the doctor-patient confidentiality oath was probably pointless. The studio's expectations—and money—were above pithy rules.

But truth be told, Charles wasn't about to let Bill or anyone else home in on his private sessions with Marilyn. No. He wanted her to himself. Most of all, he wanted her trust. Soon, he hoped, she'd consider him worthy enough to know her secrets. Secrets he'd protect. In the process, he'd best Greenson, show him up, right along with her ex-husbands. Because Charles planned on being the first man— perhaps the only man—who would save Marilyn from her addictions and demons, and possibly worst of all, herself.

TWO

Charles knew it was too late. Too late to heed Bill's warning about letting Marilyn get under his skin. What man wouldn't find her anything less than intoxicating? But Bill had a point. Charles couldn't let future sessions derail like today. He'd get a handle on Marilyn, firmly but with tenderness.

After his impromptu meeting with Bill, he had the impression few people in Marilyn's life genuinely cared about her. He promised himself that he wouldn't lose sight of how she was used and pushed like a workhorse and how others had sold out, using their association with her for their own gains.

Such determination was necessary, especially with a stuffed envelope of cash in his coat pocket bulging against his chest. The payment Bill Stewart had dropped on his desk. Charles snatched it up after Bill left and packed up for the night. Now in his car driving home, he couldn't recall the last time he felt so unsettled. Nervous even. Was he falling into a trap? Was this how Greenson started out with Marilyn, well-meaning and professional until the money and fame swelled and crested like a tidal wave? Charles refused to make the same mistake. Despite his flimsy beginning with the actress.

He steered the Buick into the driveway of his home in Compton

half an hour later. For the rest of the night, he had to shove aside the
consuming thoughts that swirled like a merry-go-round in his mind. A
deep breath prepared him.

He fished his wedding ring from his pants pocket and slipped it
back over his finger before heading inside to his wife.

HELEN and the girls greeted him in a scene that Rockwell himself
would've been proud to capture on canvas. The three of them standing
there in the living room, wearing summer dresses and ribbons in their
curls, looked ready for a picnic. A whiff of pot roast, was it, scented the
air. Since Charles could count on one hand the number of times Helen
had the girls dolled up and dinner ready after a workday, he tensed.
Awkwardness defined his homelife on a good day. Walking into this,
caution gripped him, especially when Helen made no mention about
how late he was getting in.

Charles suspected her apricot-colored dress was new but didn't
dare comment. Her hair, curled and stacked, was a far cry from its
usual disheveled state. The crimson stain on her lips transported
Charles back to the first time he saw her, singing and slinking against a
piano at The Diamond Club. In the eight years since, their sponta-
neous, fiery connection had become a heap of ashes in a stone-cold
fireplace.

Charles committed to playing out the charade but churned within.
After a trying, rousing day, he needed the numbing atmosphere he was
used to. He lacked the energy for a performance but pushed through.
Spurred on, perhaps, by the unexpected flare up of attraction that
sparked for his wife at the sight of her tonight.

"Dinner's ready." Helen clasped her hands while Charles returned
the hugs and affections from Judith and Natalie.

"Terrific. I'm starving."

They migrated to the dining room. Charles carried Natalie, tucking
strands of her auburn hair behind her little ears. Chatty and whip-
smart, Charles did his best to keep up with her four-year-old imagina-
tion and questions. Judith, a somber contrast to her sister's vivacious-

ness, was the one Charles worried about. Deeply sensitive, the six-year-old's emotions tossed her through extremes like a ragdoll. Often, she bit her nails to the quick, and if worry could be counted as a character trait, Judith had it in spades. Charles noticed she held a fistful of his jacket. He ran a hand over her platinum locks hoping to soothe her tensions. She responded by glancing up at him and smiling.

At the table, Charles peeled off the girls, who obediently took their seats under their mother's gentle command. Further astounding Charles was the way Helen maneuvered the drop-leaf cart he'd never seen her use. She filled and served everyone's plate with a contentment he didn't recognize. The chair helped steady him. To subdue his reactions, he began forking in the pot roast and vegetables.

"Mm. It's delicious." Speaking with his mouth a little too full made the girls giggle.

"It's your mother's recipe," Helen replied.

"Oh?"

"Yes, we had a wonderful conversation today, although I'm sure the telephone bill will be a small fortune." She smiled.

"Nana said she wants us to come for Christmas!" Natalie said.

"Could we, Daddy?" Judith asked, matching Natalie's zeal.

"I didn't make any promises," Helen interrupted, her smile still intact, "but I'm sure we could. Depending on what our schedules are like, but it could be managed."

And there it was. A subtle hint. The beginning of Helen's explanation for the night's pretense. *Depending on our schedules.* Charles read through that like a kindergarten primer. *Our* schedules. Helen had no schedule. Not in the sense that he did with his practice. At least, not at the moment—but she had something in mind. Helen was planning. The evening was a cheap ruse meant to soften the blow.

Charles shifted his eyes to his plate. He couldn't stand seeing the glisten of excitement in his girls' faces, knowing their hopes would be shattered. When Christmas came and there was no trip to Grandma's house, they'd be heartbroken. She wouldn't ease their disappointment. No, she'd be the cause of their misery, just like always.

"We'll see." Charles chewed his food with fortitude, knowing it was the only way to dull his anger and to keep from yelling at his wife.

WITHOUT A DOUBT, CHARLES' neighbors, Ted and Al in particular, would ridicule him if they ever caught a glimpse of Charles in the kitchen, with his sleeves rolled up, apron adorned and up to his elbows in dishwater. He found it soothing. Scrubbing away food stains brought a strange satisfaction. Perhaps it was a testament to the void of genuine, physical satisfaction in his marriage bed. Maybe there was a woman out there who could love and appreciate a man who found pleasure in the mundane. Was this the kind of *normal* Marilyn was aching for? Maybe he was a cad for getting his jollies from such thoughts. But it was all he had.

Leaving the dishes to dry on the counter, he checked on the girls and found them playing in their room. Frustration ruffled him though he should've known Helen would flit off and do her own thing. It was late, and he told the girls to get ready for bed. While they changed, and with no sign of Helen around, Charles hid the envelope of money in a shoebox on the top shelf of his bedroom closet.

Then he returned to the girls and climbed into Natalie's bed, making them giggle with delight. They rattled off the dozen items they wanted for Christmas and asked him what New Jersey was like and if they had Christmas trees and snow. He promised there was plenty of Christmas trees and snow. With Natalie snuggled next to him, he read *The Cat in The Hat* while Judith combed his hair and listened. After playfully rubbing his whiskers against their cheeks and getting good night kisses, Charles tucked them in. Every ounce of strife left him.

However, it returned when he glimpsed the dining room and realized he forgot to clean the table and drop-leaf cart. As he resumed his domestic duties, he replayed the session with Marilyn in his mind. Tomorrow would be better, he told himself. They had broken the ice, meaning the hard part was over.

Suddenly, he felt Helen there, standing in the doorway. There was no denying that Helen had presence. When she walked into a room gentlemen took note. Ladies sat a little straighter and flinched with jealousy. Although her beauty could rival Ava Gardner's, her moods were as predictable as the San Andreas Fault Line, with similar results.

"Dinner was nice." Helen had an uncelebrated talent for stating the obvious.

"Yes," Charles said flatly. Without looking at her, he moved past her and into the kitchen, where he started drying the dishes resting on the counter.

She followed him but made no move to help him.

Silence polluted the air between them.

"I'm trying, Charles."

Her remark almost made him pause and launch into an argument. *One dinner does not equate to trying*, he wanted to yell. But his girls were only steps away. He wouldn't splinter their peace. Instead, he wiped the dish in his hands to a squeaky clean.

"And I've been thinking...."

He shut his eyes. Beneath the deep breath he drew in, he warned himself against an outburst.

"They're having auditions for *My Fair Lady* over in Culver City. And The Peacock Lounge, in Lynwood, they're looking for a nightly singer."

Charles stopped wiping. "And you thought you'd do both." His turn for stating the obvious, sans the talent.

"I can do it, Charles, if you'll just support me and give me a chance."

Support? He'd given her everything a woman could want, from a beautiful home and family to stability and the freedom to shop as she pleased. And he continued to support her, even though she chose being dissatisfied over caring about the life they built for their children. How many times had he rescued laundry from the clothesline—at night—or picked up groceries or brushed the girls' hair, all in an attempt to lessen the *inconvenience* motherhood and family life had put on her? His support never faltered, even when she gave up on their relationship and cast aside his love, because his adoration couldn't compete with her desire for stardom. Helen never said it, but he suspected she married him in a moment of weakness. That she realized too late how a daily routine watered down romance and shackled her to responsibilities. The antitheist, Charles learned, to her dreams, and the one role she didn't want.

"Besides," she said, "there isn't anything to fuss over yet. I have to get the part, then we can argue."

"Is that supposed to humor me, Helen?" He turned to face her. "Let's say you get the part, and you get to headline the club. What comes next in this great plan of yours?"

"Nothing definite, Charles, you know that. But it can open the door of possibilities."

"Yes, Helen, the possibility you'll be *discovered*. Again."

Working weekends as a waitress a couple years back, Helen met a man who claimed to be a director set to film a project on Catalina Island. All he needed was a female lead, and from the instant he saw Helen, he believed she was the one. Charles told her it was a sham and forbade her to go, but she ran off with the man anyway. A week later she returned home, after the director abandoned her and disappeared with the five hundred dollars in tip money she *loaned* him.

The reminder served a cheap shot, but Charles didn't care.

"I won't let that happen again." Helen's confidence came through sharply.

Charles pointed a finger at her. "And let's not forget what you put us through afterward."

Shortly after the ruse, Helen sank into a depression, then rebounded with a strange shoplifting stint that baffled Charles.

"The answer is no, Helen. I won't set my family up for another debacle. Our girls deserve better."

"Charles, please. The shoplifting charges were dropped and—"

"I said no! Your place is here, at home with the girls like a proper mother." The notch of anger in his tone aimed to finalize the conversation.

Helen seemed aware of the fact. She slouched in the doorway as her perkiness faded. Her defeated posture didn't last. Moments later, she straightened and left the kitchen. Then, the front door opened and slammed shut with a defiant gusto that only Helen could muster.

Charles gripped the edge of the countertop to steady himself while he resisted the impulse to smash every dish in the house onto the linoleum floor.

HE CHECKED on the girls and found them undisturbed. Had they slept through the raised voices or grown accustomed to the Campbell family turmoil? A peaceful hush dominated their room. Natalie snuggled her Raggedy Ann doll. Judith clutched her mint green blanket. To fall asleep each night, she sucked and chewed on a corner. Charles couldn't get her to stop, couldn't sneak the blanket away. Now, he left it alone, no longer set on taking away her means of finding serenity. Gently, he eased the door shut and retreated into the family room.

He wouldn't wait up for Helen. In all likelihood, she'd gone to the Pub-n-Grub about four blocks away. No matter how late it got, he wouldn't show his face there, looking like an owner searching for a lost dog that had broken from its leash—or worse, a husband appearing desperate. If she wanted to drown her disappointment with shots of whiskey, he didn't care.

What he did care about was how Helen would punish him. She may have stormed out, but he knew she would exact revenge for not giving in and letting her have her way.

He put his focus elsewhere. Mopped the kitchen floor and tidied the living room. When he came across the latest edition of LIFE Magazine he was taken aback. Weakness crawled up his legs and forced him to sink onto the tufted sofa. Mesmerized, he held the periodical as if it were the Holy Grail.

Marilyn was featured on the cover.

Engulfed in a blue terrycloth robe, she was wet, poolside, and arching her back as though she was enjoying a hearty laugh. Charles flipped through the pages, and when he came to the featured section, he nearly gasped.

She was naked.

Not naked in a full-frontal sense. Unfortunately. But naked and slipping into that terrycloth robe. Forcing his eyes from the images, Charles read how Marilyn had been fired from the set of *Something's Got to Give*, just like Bill had shared. The photo was one of many taken of her during the shooting of a pool scene, where she swam naked. The article echoed more of what Bill had stated: Marilyn was habitually late or didn't show for filming or was too ill to work. However, according to the article, the last straw came for producers when Marilyn appeared at President Kennedy's nationally televised birthday celebration and sang, "Happy Birthday, Mr. President," after the film's executives had advised against it.

The photos were titillating. Not as revealing as the pictures published years earlier in that *Playboy* magazine, but these images were fresh. Marilyn was aware of her body, aware of the camera and the thousands of eyes that would be upon her.

Charles put the magazine aside and ignored the speed of his pulse. Marilyn wasn't just a goddess on a movie screen anymore. Or a beautiful woman confined to the pages of a magazine. She was going to be in his office tomorrow afternoon. How could he sit there and salivate?

But how could he not?

Needs crept over him, the kind that threaten when a man's been shunned by his wife in the bedroom for too long.

How would he withstand Marilyn's flirtations? After all, she'd kissed his cheek when she left today. He had to ignore her natural charms and remind himself that she wasn't there for him personally. She needed his help. If nothing else, Charles had a fair share of experience at putting the needs of others above his own desires. This would be no different, he assured himself. Except, if he failed Marilyn, would she take her life? His main priority was to determine if she was on the brink of another suicide attempt. A tremble passed through him as he headed for bed and a night of fitful sleep.

ONE CUP of Folger's wasn't enough for Charles the next morning, but after he made and wrapped peanut butter sandwiches for the girls, with the crusts cut off, he dashed to the office early, in no mood to spar with Helen in her hangover mode.

Later, he'd telephone Mrs. Winston across the street and ask her if she could look in on Helen and the girls. Their usual exchange would follow. Helen wasn't feeling well, and if it wasn't too much trouble could she...oh, yes, of course...she always enjoyed seeing the girls...and

Helen. Mrs. Winston was among the few who understood the thread-bare structure of Charles' family life. She didn't pry with questions or gossip with the neighbors. Charles appreciated the older woman and the fact he could focus on work for the day ahead.

He didn't have much on his morning schedule, which allowed him time to flip through the file on Marilyn that Bill Stewart had given him last week. In particular, he reviewed the information about her suicide attempts. According to the documents, she overdosed on pills three separate times. 1950, 1959, and in 1960. No mention was noted about circumstances in her life, or what might have pushed her into a state of hopelessness. It concerned Charles. She came close to dying three times. Help had reached her in time—except that wasn't true. Charles knew from his professional experience, those who tried to end their lives repeatedly were eventually successful. Plumbing into the depths of her psyche promised to be dangerous.

"Marilyn wasn't wrong about being dangerous."

Charles scribbled out a loose agenda for his session with Marilyn. Medications. Sleep. The film. He hesitated on the last item, recalling the article from LIFE Magazine and her lack of professionalism on set. Marilyn had been in films for over a decade. Was she *unmanageable* because she didn't want to act anymore? In the magazine's photographs, though, she didn't appear unmanageable. She looked incandescent, vibrant from the attention, and in damn good form.

The first two morning appointments became a blur for Charles. He mindlessly jotted notes, said little, and watched the clock. Mrs. Trippett, his third appointment, raised her head from the couch and flashed him an annoyed look when Charles didn't control the tapping of his pencil on his notepad.

Before Marilyn was due to arrive, Charles checked himself in the bathroom located down the corridor. He splashed his face with cold water. A feeble attempt to settle his infatuation but worth a try.

Back in his office, he dug into the bottom desk drawer and retrieved the old Edison reel-to-reel tape recorder he'd utilized in the earlier years of his practice. He wasn't sure why he hadn't thought of it yesterday, but going forward, he'd record his sessions with Marilyn. Then he could play back that breathy voice, take in every word she said. More importantly, he could commit to a deeper analysis of insights she shared.

He tested the buttons but didn't bother to listen to what information the tape already held. There was no time.

Once again, his wedding ring hid in his pants pocket. After last night's go-round with Helen and the fact she didn't crawl into bed until 3:24 that morning, he felt no guilt.

Precisely at 1pm, Marilyn burst into the room. Right on time but Charles thought she looked distraught. Her curls hung down into her eyes. Wrinkles marred her seafoam-colored dress. Her cheeks were flushed. Considering the summertime warmth, Charles didn't understand why she had on a trench coat, loose and falling from one shoulder.

"It's good to see you, Dr. Charlie." A tentative smile crossed her bare lips.

"Nice to see you, too, Miss Monroe." Charles guarded his reaction, not wanting to stress her further. "You seem a bit rushed today. Can I get you anything?"

"Thank you, no." Her eyes darted to the inner office. "Would you mind if I used your telephone?"

Bafflement under control, he replied, "Please help yourself."

She thanked him again and took to the office, without closing the door completely. Charles wondered if that was intentional. He heard her dial a stream of numbers, frantically.

Having never been in the position of waiting on a client, in his own office, Charles didn't know what to do with himself. Listening in wasn't an option, was it? He considered it but couldn't do it. Instead, he fiddled with the tape reel and buttons on the recorder. Everything appeared in working order.

Over the next fifteen minutes, Marilyn dialed several numbers and had multiple conversations. Charles did his best not to listen in, even though his frustration sputtered and sparked with each new zing of the rotary. He considered poking his head in and checking on her, especially when her voice escaladed and was notched with anxiety. But Charles waited, trapped in a mire of uncertainty. Irritation spiked within him. He smoked a cigarette and reminded himself she needed compassion.

He turned his attention to the tape recorder. For sheer amusement, he placed it on an end table and angled it toward the cracked-open door of his inner office. If he attempted to record her, maybe he could decipher the conversation later. He attached the microphone and set it next to the recorder. Then he plugged in the machine and clicked the red Record button. The tape reels began to rotate. Pleased with his cleverness, though he doubted any part of her phone call would be captured, he was startled moments later when he heard Marilyn raise her voice then slam down the telephone.

Sobbing softly, she returned to Charles in the outer office. He gently took her by the shoulders.

"Are you all right, Miss Monroe?"

A hand over her eyes and her head hanging, she didn't answer. Charles glanced over her shoulder and into the inner office. The trench coat was sprawled on his desk. Smoke danced in the room. Aftermath, Charles noted, from the half dozen cigarette butts now in his desktop ashtray.

"Miss Monroe?"

When she didn't answer or acknowledge him, he wasn't sure what else to do. As thrilling as it was to touch her skin, he needed to reach her. He considered leaning in and whispering her name but didn't. Instead, he squeezed her shoulders delicately.

"Oh, Dr. Campbell." Her hand slid from her face. "I'm sorry I've made a mess of your office."

"No, it's fine. I'm just concerned about you. What's happened?" He motioned to the grass-green couch for them to sit. Marilyn sat with him and seemed to be emerging from her fog of oblivion. Charles handed her a box of tissues.

"It's so complicated and wonderful and awful." She dabbed her eyes. "I'm afraid you wouldn't understand."

He doubted her intent was to sound condescending, but it peeved him anyway. "I've been working with clients for many years, Miss Monroe. There isn't much that surprises me. Besides, I'm here to help you."

"Thank you for letting me use your telephone. I'll reimburse you for the charges."

"Oh, that isn't necessary."

Her tears had smudged her eye make-up. She seemed doll-like and fragile when she looked at him.

"The telephone at my house is bugged."

Charles was wrong; he could be surprised.

"It's that Mr. Hoover," she continued, her energy apparently reviving, "you know, the man who runs the FBI? He doesn't care for some of the people I know, so he's always listening in, trying to see if I'm a communist or something. I think he even has people inside my house."

J. Edgar Hoover, inceptionist and stalwart leader of the FBI, in his mission to safeguard the country against any growing empathy toward communism or communist supporters, had become infected by his own self-appointed powers. Celebrities and politicians were his primary targets of interest, including President Kennedy and his brother Bobby. Odd, Charles thought, given the fact Kennedy had approved of an operation last year to overthrow Fidel Castro, the dictator of Cuba. Which had failed miserably and become an embarrassment to the Kennedy administration.

At one point Arthur Miller, Marilyn's former husband, had been under suspicion and was forced to testify before the House of Un-American Activities Committee in 1956 about his political activities. When he refused to name fellow co-horts, he was found guilty of contempt, sentenced to pay a $500 fine, and denied a renewed passport. Although the conviction was overturned two years later, being blacklisted hurt Miller's career.

"I think Mr. Hoover needs to get a lady of his own and stop worrying so much about what other people are doing," Marilyn added.

"You mentioned yesterday that you're dangerous. Does that have anything to do with Hoover?"

"Yes." She sounded impressed and her eyes grew wide. "I know things. I have some very special friends who tell me things, things that wouldn't be good for the public to know. It might cause a panic."

Charles didn't know whether she was spinning a yarn or being earnest. He gave her the benefit of the doubt. "And you think there's someone in your house?"

Marilyn nodded. "At night. Sometimes I hear noises outside, and sometimes it sounds like someone's in the house. But I'm always too afraid to look. I wouldn't know what to do or how to confront someone. So I stay in my room with the door locked."

"Have you considered calling the police? It could be an intruder or a rabid fan of yours."

She leaned against the couch and let the back of her head rest on the top edge. "I've never had any problems with fans. Only husbands. Sometimes I wonder if it could be Joe."

"Your ex-husband Joe?"

Another nod.

Gossip magazines had a field day with Marilyn and former Yankees slugger Joe DiMaggio. From their surprise elopement to their sudden divorce nine months later, they provided ample material for much of 1954. Reports swirled that the retired baseball star had a wicked temper, enhance by his indulgence with alcohol and triggered whenever Marilyn had to film what he considered to be, sexy scenes. Director Billy Wilder staged a late-night promotional shoot for *The Seven Year Itch* outside the Trans-Lux Theater in Manhattan that recreated her stroll across a subway grate in the iconic white dress. While the stunt exhilarated reporters, Joe DiMaggio became outraged. His fury led to an altercation with Marilyn in the theater lobby. Witnesses described the scene as a "yelling battle." One month later, Marilyn filed for divorce.

But DiMaggio didn't leave her alone. He hired a private investigator to follow her, and when the investigator reported one night that Marilyn was visiting a potential new lover, Joe took action. He telephoned several pals, including Frank Sinatra, and hightailed it to the modest apartment complex where Marilyn was purportedly in the arms of another man. Joe and his posse broke down the apartment door—using an ax—and awoke Miss Florence Ross. No criminal charges were filed, but Miss Ross, traumatized from the ordeal, sued for damages and won. Marilyn and her friend Sheila, in the apartment next door, were unaware of what happened until later.

When the press caught wind of the incident, they dubbed it *The Wrong Door Raid*. Joe suffered no consequences for his reckless behavior, and his intentions about what he planned to do if he found Marilyn, were never made clear.

A chill slithered over Charles as he dared to imagine DiMaggio confronting Marilyn with that ax in his hands. Even though years had passed since the events, he believed Marilyn's concerns about Joe were valid.

"From what I've read, he wasn't good to you." Charles hoped the remark wouldn't rile and renew her agitation from earlier.

"He didn't understand Hollywood. I suppose it's hard for people who aren't in the business. You spend a lot of time creating a fantasy. At least, that's what they have me do. Joe didn't like other men looking at me. He said it was vulgar."

Charles wondered if DiMaggio had seen the picture spread in LIFE.

"If the police caught Joe lurking around your house, I'm sure the press would turn it into a circus. You don't need that kind of attention right now, but Marilyn, you must protect yourself." Charles resisted the urge to put his hand atop her knee or on her shoulder. "Promise me, please, that if you think someone is in your home, you'll call the police."

Marilyn. He'd called her by her first name, without asking her permission. Another professional faux pas. But saying her name felt natural. And electrifying.

"Maybe you're right." She dropped her handful of wrinkled tissues into the wastebasket near the side of the couch and seemed not to notice Charles' gaffe. "But everything's going to work out, I just need to be patient and wait. Just a little while longer. You know something, soon the whole world's going to be jealous of me."

"To be honest, I think many already are."

"Well, this is different. I'm going to be extremely happy." Her luminous glow returned and erased the signs of her crying.

"That's what everyone wants for you, Marilyn. People want you happy, healthy, able to work."

"Oh, I won't have to worry about movies and studios anymore. I'm going to be getting married!"

"Married?" The revelation hit like a kick to the gut. "I didn't realize you were in a serious relationship."

"It's a secret." She stood, then twirled once, like a little girl showing off a new dress. "I'm very good at keeping secrets."

Yes, you've alluded to that.

Charles couldn't explain why, but his stomach knotted. Secrets were one thing, delusions another.

"We're friends now, and I hope you realize you don't have to keep any secrets from me." He hated sounding desperately curious, but Marilyn hadn't proven to be as chatty as he'd hoped. "The best way for me to help you is if I know more about you, about what concerns you, and what's happening in your private life."

"It's complicated, but the best romances always are."

"Like your relationship with Yves?" Charles cringed after the unfiltered comment escaped him. Who was he to be so bold? So careless?

Marilyn and Yves Montand, her suave co-star in *Let's Make Love*, had an affair during filming. Both were married at the time. Ironically, if one believed the speculation, their spouses, Arthur and Simone Signoret also enjoyed each other's intimate company. When the film wrapped, the affairs fizzled. Hollywood in a nutshell.

Charles feared the thoughtless remark would injure her budding trust in him, but Marilyn flashed that coy smile of hers.

"I wasn't in love with Yves," she said. "Not like this." She twirled again, added a few steps at the end, probably from one of her dance numbers. "But you're right, the man I'm seeing—the man I love—he is married."

"Quite a complication."

"That's only part of the problem," Marilyn continued. "He doesn't love his wife anymore. I think he was forced into marrying her. All she cares about is his money—and he's so very wealthy! For now we have to be careful, and we can't be together too often. The press might find out."

"Yes, I imagine—"

"Can I trust you, Charlie?" Marilyn fell onto her knees in front of Charles and placed her hands on his knees. "*Really* trust you?"

The sudden closeness challenged his ability to think straight.

"Uh, why of course," he managed, though not without a slight crack in his voice.

"You might as well know everything about me. This will be hard for you to understand, and I know you might not believe me, but I'm going to be the next first lady! Isn't that wonderful? I'm in love with the president!"

THREE

arry the president!

Clearly, this woman had greater problems than pills, lack of sleep, or losing her job—or even worries that Hoover was watching her. Marilyn Monroe or not, how could she possibly believe that President Kennedy would divorce his wife and marry her?

Charles had trouble focusing. She popped to her feet and carried on about how exasperated Kennedy was with his wife's spending, on both the White House restoration and her personal wardrobe. Somewhere in her rambling, she mentioned that she had even warned Jackie Kennedy that her marriage was over.

"I'm sorry, Marilyn, but did you say you've spoken with Jackie Kennedy?"

"Yes! I called the White House, her private number. I was a little drunk I think, but I told her it was all over, that Johnny wasn't in love with her anymore and that he wants to be with me."

"Johnny?"

Charles couldn't help repeating it, although the tone of the nickname struck him like an out of tune violin. Marilyn did that pleased-with-herself, girlish shrug of hers. She continued her dance steps, tapping her feet, swaying softly, turning, all to a mild rhythm apparently in her head and happily oblivious to the damage that could be unleashed, if her story were true. Charles rubbed his forehead as if that could settle the confusion tearing through his mind.

"What was Mrs. Kennedy's reaction to this?" Charles asked.

"Nothing much really. I don't think she believed me. All she said was, *Yes, Marilyn you're going to move into the White House and all these problems will be yours.* I thought it was a funny thing to say. Maybe she'd been drinking. Johnny wasn't happy with me and didn't like that I called, but I thought I was doing him a favor, since he hadn't told her. Men don't always know how to handle women. I said it would be best to simply tell her straight."

Charles reached for a cigarette and offered Marilyn a smoke. She accepted and rejoined him on the couch. Charles placed an ashtray between them. Within minutes, a Pall Mall cloud filled the room.

"So you've been seeing the president for some time?" Charles didn't know where to lead the conversation, or if he was leading. He began to worry that Marilyn was on the verge of a breakdown of sorts.

Details from her file began to stream through his mind. In particular, her divorce from Arthur Miller in early 1961 led to a stay in New York's Payne Whitney Psychiatric Clinic. Marilyn's psychoanalyst at the time, Dr. Marianne Kris, feared Marilyn's depression would lead to suicide. Dr. Kris convinced Marilyn to check in for much needed rest and relaxation, but when she did, Marilyn was locked in a padded room for three days. When she was finally permitted to make phone calls, Marilyn telephone Joe DiMaggio, who immediately arranged her release and transfer to Columbia-Presbyterian Hospital, where she stayed for several weeks without being locked up. Afterward, Marilyn didn't take on any new film projects the rest of the year.

"I've met Johnny several times. We weren't romantic right away, but the attraction was instant. I think I met him at a party at the Lawfords' residence. You know, Peter Lawford, the actor? He's Johnny's brother-in-law."

Like most Americans, Charles knew. Few details about the Kennedys' lives remained a mystery since the election, especially their vast family tree.

"Seems like it was a fundraiser." Marilyn tapped her finger to her chin, as if that might stimulate the memory. "Johnny loves California and anything to do with movie stars. The more we saw each other, the more our attraction grew. Our passions finally took over, but it was just a few months ago when I realized that I was in love with him. We spent a weekend together, in Palm Springs. That's when Johnny said he loved me. And there was that night at the Carlyle, after the birthday party. We couldn't be alone that night. Johnny said it was too risky."

Marilyn stared off, lost in the recollection, presumably. She took a long drag on her cigarette, exhaled slowly as she seemed to enjoy the memory.

Her *Happy Birthday, Mr. President* performance at Madison Square Garden on May 19th, just weeks ago, created plenty of titillating rumors. There she was, glittering on stage in a flesh-colored gown covered with beads. Though her behavior that night ranked from playful to inebriated, everyone who witnessed the televised event had wondered if the world's most powerful man and Hollywood's favorite bombshell were playing hanky-panky behind closed doors. Jackie Kennedy's absence from the event ramped up speculation.

"I just have to remember that he loves me." Marilyn said it more to herself than to Charles. "He *loves* me." She closed her eyes and repeated the phrase softly.

Her intense concentration caused her to forget her cigarette, which tumbled from her grasp and onto the couch. Marilyn startled to attention but not before a hole was left in the fabric. Popping to her feet, she apologized profusely.

"It's nothing to worry about," Charles said, after stamping the spot with his foot to ensure there wasn't a fire. "I've been meaning to throw that old thing out. I hope it didn't ruin your dress."

Marilyn checked but found no blemish.

"Why am I so clumsy?" Her face wrinkled into a frown. "I need to go." She stepped into the inner office and snatched her coat from the desktop.

Charles wasn't sure how long their actual session had lasted, if their interaction even qualified as a session. Marilyn had been in his office for quite a while, since her dramatic arrival. He was relieved he had no other clients scheduled for the day.

"Please stay," Charles said. "There's still so much to discuss."

Marilyn shook her head. "Maybe I shouldn't be talking about this. I'm so clumsy and I ruin everything, it's true." In a half-mad attempt to shrug the trench on and over her shoulders, two pill bottles fell from the pockets.

Charles knelt to retrieve them and couldn't help reading the labels. Nembutal. Barbiturates prescribed by Greenson.

"Marilyn, you do know you must be careful with these?" Charles held up the bottles.

She took them and placed them back into her pockets.

"Yes." Her voice barely above a whisper, she went toward the door. "Thank you, Dr. Charlie. You've been very kind. I don't know what I would've done without you today."

Charles wanted to beg her to stop, to stay, explain. Mostly, he wanted to grab the bottles of pills and throw them out the window, concerned over how many she might be taking.

Damn you, Greenson! Why are you making it easy for her to be careless and hurt herself?

Before he could say anything or his frustrations manifest, she breezed out the door.

AFTER MARILYN'S HASTY EXIT, the revelations she shared ran through Charles' head like wildfire. Was he wrong to let her leave? No. She wasn't experiencing a breakdown. If he wanted, though, Charles could've had her committed for a seventy-two-hour hold. Similar to Marilyn's previous experience, where she would have been restrained and locked in a room. Although Marilyn's statements raised his concerns, he wouldn't risk destroying the faith she had in him.

Keeping secrets was one thing, being delusional was another. Because it couldn't be true, could it? Affair or not, the idea of President Kennedy leaving his wife for Marilyn Monroe—in the middle of his term—was preposterous. Perhaps this was what she meant when she told Charles she was dangerous. If the scandal unfolded the way Marilyn expected, the United States would be disgraced. Charles didn't know the exact political ramifications but imagined they would be horrific.

Charles remembered the tape recorder. It had shut off after reaching the end of the reel. He clicked the rewind button and waited several seconds before pushing play. Marilyn's voice trilled out: *"...Palm Springs. That's when Johnny said he loved me."*

Charles turned it off, folded over the recorder's hinged top, with the microphone inside and put it back in his desk drawer after unplugging it. He'd captured Marilyn, in her own words, admitting to an affair with Kennedy. Although it wasn't the same as having photographic proof of them together, it was close enough for Charles. Possessing a recording of her outlining details of their relationship suddenly made him nervous. He didn't want to think about what could happen if the tape got into the wrong hands.

Dangerous indeed.

HE LOCKED the office and headed to Oscar's, a trendy bar within walking distance. Despite the storm in his head, Charles thought of his father when he slid onto the barstool. A brick layer by trade, George Campbell took to drinking like a Wallenda to a highwire. On a regular night, he came home with three or four beers under his belt, to his wife's chagrin. That's what it took to keep him level, George had once said so himself. It was the nights when countless drinks passed over his pallet that made tranquility at home brittle.

Because of his father, Charles wasn't much of a drinker. He determined never to let his wife and girls see him wobble in the door or be ruled by a saucy temper. For the most part, he avoided alcohol. A wise choice considering Helen's moods and temperament. But today, he needed a beer.

Charles shoved his father and his wife from the forefront of his mind. He went over his exchange with Marilyn and tried to make better sense of all she'd shared.

The telephone calls she made from his office that afternoon, had she been contacting President Kennedy? Is that what had taken her so long, trying to reach her lover, who was busy tending to world affairs, or even his own family? Charles had heard bits of Marilyn's conversation through the cracked-open door. *Did you tell him it's Mrs. Green calling? Again? Have you given him my messages?* Was that a secret code between Marilyn and the president? Or was she attempting to get a hold of Bobby Kennedy? Was he the one who arranged their rendezvous?

Such supposition could drive a man crazy, Charles thought, and he could see the strain the situation was putting on Marilyn. In his opinion, she wasn't a woman who could handle an elaborate deception or one who embraced subtly.

Charles worried for her. What would happen when she let the details of the affair slip to the wrong person? Plus, Charles couldn't help wondering what Kennedy told Marilyn during their liaisons. Was he leading her on, making false promises just for the sake of keeping their trysts light and playful? Obviously, the man had given no thought to Marilyn's wellbeing. Sooner or later, he imagined, Kennedy would toss her aside. Resentment swelled inside Charles.

He'd be there for her, as much as she'd allow him and trust him, but he wondered if that would be enough. Because if Kennedy broke off the affair, Charles knew she would be shattered. He hoped beyond hope that she would confide in him and come to him instead of relying on the comfort and oblivion of the pills.

A HEARTY SLAP landed on his shoulder, starting him to attention at the arrival of his friend, Bertrand Miller. They greeted one another as Bert helped himself to the stool beside Charles.

"How's that pretty wife of yours treatin' you these days?" Bert tossed back his head and shook a handful of beer nuts into his mouth.

Charles suppressed the inward groan that rose up at the mention of Helen. He delivered a dutiful comment that the family was well and good. Bert probably knew better but didn't press.

Bert's intuitiveness was inescapable since he and Charles had grown up together in New Jersey. Although Bert's facial features resembled a young Humphrey Bogart, he lacked Bogart's charisma but made up for it with a scrappy, first-to-jump-into-the-fight attitude. Back in high school, when Charles told him he was trading the East coast for the West coast, Bert joined him. One semester at Berkley convinced him that he wasn't a college man. Bouncing around jobs for a few years, he found a fit as a private investigator. Although some people looked down upon his hustle of tailing cheating spouses and digging into people's lives to expose secrets, Bert didn't care. He told Charles the money afforded him a decent place to live and enabled him to be a regular at The Blue Velvet Room, a *gentleman's* club. He didn't need much else.

"Business good these days?" Charles preferred to change the subject, not only to avoid the topic of Helen but also because he liked Bert's crazy stories. Tales about catching a politician with a hooker or taking a beating in a back alley proved entertaining.

"Same as always." Bert dropped his favorite expletive. "So what's going on? You sounded spooked over the phone, and it's too early for Halloween."

Before leaving the office, Charles had called Bert. Hearing Marilyn's admission of an affair with President Kennedy had made Charles edgy, and he started to wonder: if Hoover was keeping tabs on Marilyn and her activities, was he next?

"I've got a new client, an actress, and I might need some help with her."

A mischievous smirk appeared as Bert lit into a cigarette.

"Is this gonna be like that last time?"

Charles hoped that in the dimmed lighting of Oscar's, his embarrassment didn't show. Before Helen had turned their life upside-down with the shoplifting stunt at Bullock's Department Store, Charles had found a pleasing distraction from his marital woes with his dry cleaner's daughter.

He'd been an idiot, carrying on with that young girl. The so-called relationship had nowhere to go, especially since Charles had no intention of domesticating the girl or leaving Helen. More than feeling guilty or ashamed, he hated that he turned into a cliché. Once his needs were satisfied, and a fear of discovery began to override his desires, Charles ended it before Helen found out.

"No." Charles said it without looking at his friend. "It's nothing like that."

"Good, 'cause I ain't so good with lying to your wife."

Charles had used Bert several times as an alibi during the affair. Heat raced to his face as the memories surfaced.

"Please tell me this new client is that Ursula Andress." Bert's eyebrows shot up, hopeful.

"I can't tell you who she is, you know that, and trust me, it's for your own good."

"This I gotta hear." Bert ordered a double shot of bourbon.

Charles gave Bert a censored outline of recent events. He told him about being approached by a studio executive, about how the actress was troubled, and possibly taking too many medications. Charles' biggest concern, he shared, was the fact that the woman was under government surveillance, and he worried he might be too.

Bert kept quiet a moment then stamped out his cigarette.

"I ain't a genius, Chuck, but it don't take one of them nuclear scientists to piece together who you're talking about."

"Don't worry about drawing conclusions." Charles hoped his bland expression confirmed or denied nothing. "I need you to do me a favor."

"Figures." Bert signaled the bartender for another round.

"I wonder if you could dig around for me, see what you find."

"Hard to do if I'm not given any names."

Charles didn't relent.

"What exactly am I looking for?" Bert asked.

"The guy from the studio, Bill Stewart, start with him. See if he has any ties to Hoover. I want to know if I'm being used or set up."

Bert gave a slight chuckle. "Because it's just that easy."

"It should be for you. This is what you do."

"I don't mess with no G-men."

"Consider it a chance to broaden your skills," Charles said.

"Why you, Chuck? All the doctors in this town, why'd you get picked for this job?"

"I've started wondering the same thing." Charles drained what remained of his beer. "Look, Bert, you're the only person I can trust with this."

Bert nodded. "I'm on it, and you know I'll do you a solid. Maybe I should come by your office one afternoon, you know, discuss any findings. You know a good time I should drop by?" Bert wiggled his eyebrows.

Charles picked up his hat from the bartop and placed it snug around his head.

"You might want to hold off on that visit, Bert. She's a dangerous woman, if you know what I mean."

KEEPING to his one beer limit, and resisting Bert's encouragement for one more, Charles paid his tab and headed home. He'd be earlier than last night, much earlier, but he wasn't anxious to face Helen after last night's episode. With that in mind, he let the Buick glide on the streets slowly. He had the girls to consider though. Perhaps Charles had been irresponsible, leaving them with their mother hungover, but he was tired of trying to make things easy for Helen. Her selfishness infuriated him, especially when it came to the girls, and he absolutely wouldn't tolerate a discussion about Helen performing while she made such little effort with her daughters.

When he walked into the house, silence greeted him. He called out, but the slapping of little feet on the floor didn't respond. Neither did Helen.

Muffled sounds from the bathroom prickled his attention. He knocked and pushed the door open. Helen stood in front of the sink with curlers piled in her hair and make-up brazen enough for a clown. She wore a short black robe, similar to the kind found at a downtown salon. Charles couldn't resist wondering if she had stolen it from such an establishment.

"Oh, you're home already?" Helen turned down the radio sitting atop the commode. The noise Charles had heard. "I thought I'd try this new style." A magazine lay open on the closed toilet lid. If it was the recent edition of LIFE, Charles couldn't tell.

"Helen, where are the girls?"

"Playing, I guess." She spoke as though she'd misplaced an earring.

"You don't leave a six- and four-year-old to play by themselves, Helen! They're children!"

"I haven't left them!" A pink sponge curler tumbled from her hair as she stood toe-to-toe with her husband. "I've been right here, all day!"

Charles grabbed her by the shoulders.

"All you ever think about is yourself!!"

"What are you talking about?" She shrugged hard to escape his grasp and pushed him away. "I gave up everything for you, for the girls! I could've had my big break by now, but I threw it away. And for what?" Tears glistened in her eyes. "I could've been happy!"

"Those girls deserve better than you!"

Helen slapped him.

"Mommy?" came a small voice from behind them.

Charles and Helen turned and saw their daughters, eyes wide with trepidation and a plate in each of their hands.

"What's this?" Charles asked, ignoring the sting to his face.

"Mommy was busy," Natalie said. "So we made dinner." She pressed her lips together and forced a grin.

Charles noticed that Judith's plate trembled. He knelt and put his hand underneath it for support. Distress swam in Judith's eyes, the way it always did when conflict flared between her parents. Charles waited a moment and let her focus on his reassuring smile. She gave an unsteady grin in return.

"Where were you girls?" he asked gently but with concern.

"We took a plate to Mrs. Winston," Natalie said.

"Oh. That was very thoughtful. Let's see what we have." Charles looked over the plate. Peeled orange slices, pickles, and toast. Natalie's favorite foods to eat, though not necessarily together. When Charles imagined the two of them standing on Mrs. Winston's door stoop, his chest tightened. An equal flux of pride and heartbreak rose within.

"We went to Mr. Griffith's store and got the bread and butter," Natalie added, matter-of-factly.

"Oh? You walked there by yourselves?"

Both girls nodded.

Charles looked to Judith. "How did you pay for it?"

"He said you could pay him later." Judith began to nibble on a fingernail, possibly worried an uproar was about to follow.

Humiliation pulsed through Charles. He was usually with them, holding each one by the hand, as the girls skipped their way to the neighborhood grocery. Helen made appearances, too, when the mood struck, but hardly knew where to find anything. Though Charles couldn't say that he and Niles Griffith were close, an understanding had passed between them. Or was it just sympathy that emitted from Mr. Griffith, realizing that Charles and his girls were yoked with a woman like Helen.

Without glancing back at Helen, he said, "We should get the table set and eat then. Before it gets cold."

Natalie beamed with delight and giggled. Relief washed over Judith's pale face as Charles gently ushered them to the table with his hand in the small of their backs.

"Come on, Mommy," Natalie called over her shoulder.

"I'll be right there, baby."

Charles hoped she'd take her time. He needed a moment for his frustration to loosen its grip. All he had to do was make it through dinner. Once he and Helen were alone, they'd talk. Tucked inside his pants pocket awaited a meaningful solution, one he should've resorted to long ago.

AFTER PUTTING the girls to bed, Charles and Helen returned to the kitchen. Helen sat at the dinette table and sighed as if she were weary from a busy day. Silence beat. Charles didn't bother with small talk or a lead in. He took a pill bottle from his pants pocket and set it on the tabletop, in front of Helen.

Helen, her curls now droopy and her face washed clean, stared at the bottle.

"You're not drugging me."

"There are only three tablets. One a day. It's just a trial." His tone was metered. Calm. For his sake as well as hers. "We have to try something, Helen." Charles began pacing behind her, his hands dug deep into his pockets.

Helen tilted her head slightly. "Stop pretending with me and just say it."

"What?"

"You wish you would've put me in that asylum or let me go to jail."

"That's not true." Jail or a hospital stay, he knew, would've been detrimental to Helen, and to whatever hope they had left at a mediocre marriage. Helen was neither a mental case nor a criminal. Shoplifting the perfume and earrings from Bullock's had been for attention. But Charles had hoped that threats of being locked up would straighten out Helen's behavior. Jolt her into realizing what a glorious, stable life he provided for her. Last night reaffirmed none of it had worked.

"You should've left me at the Diamond Club, Charles."

He paused and didn't feel an urge to correct her or tell her she was wrong. His mind swirled back to that club, to that image of Helen, making love to the audience with her singing and seductive moves. That tight, red-sequined dress had captivated him, almost as much as those Lauren Bacall-like stares she gave him. He wanted to possess her, and he put more thought into his pursuit of her than what it would mean for her to become his wife.

That had been his mistake, attempting to mold her into his version of the woman he wanted her to be. In his reasoning, she owed him. Because he provided. No woman in their right mind truly craved the manic life of an actress. Enslaved to an unpredictable work schedule, practically owned by a studio, while yielding to the demands of a director.

There was also the rejection to contend with. Charles had watched Helen lose that battle. She attended a handful of auditions after Natalie arrived but to no avail. Days of crying had followed, convincing

Charles she couldn't take those hits to her self-esteem and confirming what he already suspected—she wasn't cut out for the business. Helen never saw it that way.

But now, Judith and Natalie were the ones suffering, having a mother who was permanently distracted, yearning for a life that offered her greater satisfaction than the suburbs of Compton. Charles hated that he and the girls weren't enough for her.

By refusing the pills Helen was telling him that she wouldn't embrace a whatever-it-takes attitude toward preserving her family or repairing her marriage. She had no interest in trying. For Charles, it was also an indication that she didn't trust him.

Standing behind Helen he stared at her blankly. What good could come from their stalemate? Charles could feel the anxiety building within him, and worse—the burden of discontent entwined with hopelessness. Was there any way to save his family?

FOUR

Charles rose early, packed a bag for the girls, and carried them out to the Buick in the tender morning light. He placed them on their pillows, gave Natalie her Raggedy Ann doll, and told them it was okay to go back to sleep. He wasn't ready for their questions, or for Judith's fretfulness to stir his own concerns.

He left a note for Helen.

At a gas station along Route 66 he stopped and telephoned Pam, Helen's sister. Without much of an explanation, he told her he was bringing the girls to stay with her for a few days. Pam told him to drive safely and promised to have pancakes ready for them when they made it to San Bernardino. Charles managed a thank you, shaky as it was.

True to form, Pam, her husband Jim and their three kids welcomed Charles and his sleepy-eyed girls. Part of him hated seeing Jim. Although Jim genuinely adored Judith and Natalie, Charles sensed that Jim tolerated him and Helen for his wife's sake. Whenever he and Jim were partnered together in a game of canasta, they lost, and Jim ranked among one of the few men who seemed repulsed by Helen's flirtations. Needless to say, Charles wasn't disappointed that Jim ducked out the door and off to his accounting firm soon after Charles and the girls arrived.

The warm pancakes, smothered in butter and drizzled in syrup, quickly roused Judith and Natalie's energy and their smiles. When they finished, forks clattered against the plates and chair legs scraped the linoleum floor as they zipped from the table and out to the yard with their cousins, eager to play.

When they were alone, Charles gave Pam the abridged version of recent events.

"She's only going to get worse," Pam said after listening to Charles. No surprise showed on her face, perhaps a result of numbness from years of exposure to Helen's antics. Unlike her sister, Pam had a reserved nature that some construed as being standoffish. Her quiet beauty became enhanced, for Charles, the more he worked his way through her cautious, guarded layers.

From what he understood about their younger years, Pam played the role of passed-over sister to Helen's allure and charisma. Pam's knack for penetrating discernment of people and situations was often mistaken for brooding or resentment. But not by Charles. She was the sharpest woman he'd ever met—and he regretted not recognizing her warmth and strengths sooner.

"I don't know what's left to do or even try." Charles hated sounding helpless. Being in Jim's happy home only worsened the bite of ruin.

"Maybe it's time to let her go and get on with your life," Pam said.

"Divorce?"

Pam served a level gaze. "Is that the only sin you two haven't committed yet?"

Charles rubbed his hand over his face and budding whiskers. He already felt beaten down. Visiting the list of his shortcomings would only intensify his sense of failure. He took a generous drink of his coffee, attempting to mask his reddened face.

"You should save yourself and protect the girls, Charles."

He looked at them, spinning outside on the tire swing. Despite the laughter that carried into the house, Charles caught that expression of uncertainty on Judith's face when she glanced his way. He flashed his best reassuring grin while wishing he knew how to save and protect them all.

LATE THAT MORNING, back at the office, Charles nicked his chin while performing a quick shave in the restroom. He kept the blood from dripping onto his pristine-white shirt but cursed just the same. Would Helen call or show up and create a scene? Declare that he had no right to take the girls without a discussion? He knew the anticipation of her reaction would nag him all day. Worse, it would fog his mind and distract him while his patients shared their woes.

Perhaps he was a coward for taking the girls to Pam's, but he would have peace of mind knowing they were safe and getting their fill of playtime and grilled cheese sandwiches. Maybe he could sit down with Helen and have a genuine conversation this evening. One that didn't lead to a confrontation.

Charles put aside his personal issues and prepared for the day's clients. Marilyn was scheduled for another afternoon session. He had considered telephoning her last night and checking on her, but the friction in his own him prevented it.

Two patients into his day, his lack of focus mounted. Had he written the correct dosage on that last prescription he handed to Mr. Phillips? Glancing at his notepad, he realized at the end of his hour with Mrs. Fischer, that he'd done little more than doodle references to Marilyn, JFK, Bobby, and J. Edgar Hoover. Plus, he couldn't escape thinking about what Bert had asked him yesterday at the bar: *Why you?* Yes, why had he, Dr. Charles Campbell, been picked to treat Marilyn— and become plunged into the thick of world-altering gossip?

His eagerness for Marilyn's arrival had him antsy. From her entrance to her exit, and every minute in between, he had no idea what to expect. And he couldn't wait.

Once he bid Mrs. Fischer good day and reminded her that sticking to her Thorazine regiment would keep Elvis from skinny dipping in her pool, Charles remembered the tape recorder.

After the surprise visit from Bill, Charles had been anxious to escape the office and get to Oscar's. In his haste, he'd only listened to a sliver of the recording. Now, he pushed the buttons, rewinding the tape, then clicked play. After fast-forwarding a bit, he got to the section that captured Marilyn's tale. Calling Jackie Kennedy, confessing her love for JFK and details of their affair—it was all there.

The hairs on the back of his neck stood when he heard Marilyn's voice play back. Whether or not having the recording was a good thing, Charles didn't know. He turned down the volume, concerned someone else might hear. Returning to the desk drawer, he dug around and found another reel. He removed the tape with Marilyn's confession and set the machine to record again. With his fingers over the buttons, guilt began to seep over him.

I should tell her she's being taped.

But he cast the thought aside. She would lose her candor and feel on edge if she knew. Her trust in him would diminish. He decided to risk it, like he'd done yesterday. Accidentally.

When the wall clock stretched toward two, though, nearly an hour past their scheduled appointment, Charles worried. He began pacing and poking his head into the hallway that led to his office. Should he telephone her residence? Marilyn didn't strike him as the type who missed an appointment because she was busy at home.

Anxiousness racked his mind. He had no choice but to compartmentalize his frustrations when his next client showed.

Halfway through the session, Marilyn entered his inner office without knocking, draped in a trench coat, curls drooping from underneath a head scarf, and a bottle of champagne in hand.

"Oh, you're with someone." Marilyn batted her eyes and looked from Charles to Mrs. Trippett, who sat upright on the couch.

"Yes, she's my client." Charles didn't know what to say, taking in her appearance.

"Am I late?" Marilyn cocked her head sideways.

"It's fine." He helped Mrs. Trippett to her feet. "Could I please speak with you a moment in the other room, Mrs. Trippett?" He looked over his shoulder at Marilyn. "I'll be right back. Please, take a seat."

With her mouth gaping and her eyes wide with astonishment, Mrs. Trippett let Charles lead her by the hand into the outer office.

"Is that Marilyn Monroe?" she asked after Charles closed the door separating the spaces.

"No, but she does bare a resemblance. I'm sorry for the interruption, Mrs. Trippet, but I can credit it to next month's sessions."

"Why, I had no idea you were so famous, Dr. Campbell." Mrs. Trippett, flabbergasted, snatched the lapel of his jacket, as if she were thrilled to be in on a secret.

Charles doubted that knowing Marilyn qualified him as being famous. All he cared about was getting rid of Mrs. Trippett. Politely, of course. He handed the woman her purse and hat.

"Tell me, Dr. Campbell, what's she like?"

"Now, now, Mrs. Trippett. You know I can't discuss another patient with you—and don't go running to conclusions. We've talked about that, what harm can come. Remember?"

Mrs. Trippett's amusement dissipated. She squeezed her belongings as Charles opened the office door for her to leave.

"I trust you'll be fine, until our next meeting?" he asked.

She nodded absently and Charles shut the door behind her.

Returning to Marilyn, Charles found the trench coat shed onto the floor. Marilyn was bent over, presenting her derrière, lush and curvaceous in a powder blue skirt, while searching through the credenza. Another scene Charles never would have envisioned in his office.

"May I help you with something?" He forced the words over the tightness in his throat.

Marilyn popped up. Still wearing the scarf around her head, curls hung in her face. "Don't you have any glasses here?"

He was taken aback by the tinge of disbelief in her voice.

"No. I don't usually drink at the office."

"Oh. I guess we'll have to share then." She handed him the bottle of Dom Perignon.

"What's this for?"

"We forgot to celebrate my birthday!"

Her mood troubled him. The purple crescents under her eyes suggested she hadn't slept recently, which might've explained her tardiness and scattered behavior.

"Marilyn, how many pills have you taken today?"

"Just a few." She shrugged a shoulder in her fitted white top, a gesture Charles was becoming acquainted with and recognizing as a sign of vulnerability.

"Why don't we sit first." He motioned with his hand for her to join him on the couch. She did but remained rigid. "Do you know what pills you took?"

"I don't want to talk about pills, Dr. Charlie. I want to celebrate with you." She scooted closer to him.

"Marilyn, the medicines you've taken can be very dangerous, especially if you take too many."

"That's why I only took four...or six."

"Marilyn—"

"There's no need to fuss, Charlie." She put her hand on his chest. "Look how happy I am today. Did you know it was my birthday a few weeks ago?"

Now I'm simply Charlie?

"I believe so," Charles said absently.

"Open it." She glanced at the bottle like a giddy puppy, ready to play fetch.

At a loss, Charles freed the cork and felt like a schmuck as the bubbly showered his carpet. Marilyn grabbed the bottleneck and sipped the exploding fizz. She took a hearty drink, then handed it to Charles. He took a swig, foolishly hoping it would clear his mind.

"What have you been doing today, Marilyn?"

Charles had to forget the way her lips caressed the bottle top—that his mouth was practically touching hers.

"Actually, I was with Ralph this morning."

"Greenson? He saw you like this?" Charles didn't like his own tone, a mixture of incredulity and irritation, but Marilyn took back the bottle and paid no attention.

"We had breakfast, then I swam in his pool." She laughed. "He likes watching me."

Disgust thumped Charles in the chest. Was Greenson taking advantage of her, drugging her up and....? He didn't want to finish the thought.

So much for cutting ties.

Marilyn removed the scarf and shook out her hair. Unruliness best defined her 'do, but nothing it seemed, at least in Charles' mind, damp-ened her appeal.

"Does *Ralph* know about...your involvement with Johnny?" Charles felt awkward referring to the president as Johnny. Even more troubling was lending a sliver of validation to the depth of her connection with the man.

"Oh, I've told him everything. He thinks a healthy relationship is just what I need."

"He considers you having an affair with the married president *healthy?*"

"People do have their opinions, but soon it won't matter."

"You've mentioned that." Charles had to mask his impatience better. "What does it mean? Has he made you promises?"

"Oh, Charlie, you'll see." Suddenly, Marilyn swiveled her bum on the couch and fell backwards with her head landing in Charles' lap. "Everything's going to work out." She stared up at him, then shifted her head as she reached for the cut on Charles' chin. "What's this?"

"Shaving accident." His voice quivered. How could it not with her head in his lap, touching him like he belonged to her? Was she like this with most men, or was it the effect of too much medication? Or a buzz from the champagne?

He took in the sight of her in his lap. It was like a dream, like looking at a goddess, the reality of her too much. But then, Charles saw it: a yellowish-green mark at the side of her cheek. He slid his fingertips over it, seeing if it would smudge. The mark remained. Was it a fading bruise? Charles noticed another discoloration on her collar-bone, more severe in color than the other.

"Marilyn, where did you get these bruises? Who's been hurting you?" It was a brazen assumption on his part, but he'd seen it before. Patients who were committed to staying in abusive relationships, and patients who hurt themselves.

"No one," she whispered, then turned her head toward his belly button.

"You can tell me. Was it Greenson? Kennedy? Or,,,Joe?"

"It's not like that. Oh, you wouldn't understand, Charlie."

She sat up and reached for the champagne. Tilting her head back, she held the bottle above her mouth and poured. She began to laugh, which seemed to affect her concentration. Drizzles of bubbly raced down her face and neck. She wiped away the traces and fell back into Charles' lap, still laughing. He knew the antic was an intentional ploy to change the subject and lessen the seriousness of her allegations with the president.

"Charles?"

He snapped his head up at the sound of Helen's voice.

"What are you doing here?"

Marilyn lifted her head and tried sitting up. Charles gave her a firm but gentle lift as he stood. His jaw went slack, not only from Helen's surprise visit but also from her striking appearance. She wore a Christian Dior suit he had purchased for one of her birthdays. A gift she opened but never tried on. Not when he was around.

Helen seemed to take stock of the scene. She scanned over the discarded trench on the floor and champagne, but her gaze became transfixed on Marilyn and her disheveled hair.

"Miss Monroe," Helen said with a measure of sweetness and surprise. "It's a pleasure to meet you. I'm Ellen Taylor." She gave special emphasis to *Ellen*.

Charles felt his jaw drop another notch, hearing her introduce herself as someone else. And not admitting that she was his wife.

"You're an actress, too?" Marilyn asked, perkily.

"Yes."

There it was, Charles thought. Helen wanted Marilyn to have the impression that the two of them were of the same caliber. Contemporaries, even.

"Oh, I thought you looked familiar. And you see Dr. Charlie?" Marilyn fiddled with her curls as if there was hope of taming them.

The Dr. Charlie remark caught Helen's attention. She arched an eyebrow Charles' way, but only enough that he would notice.

"You could say that."

"He's wonderful, isn't he?"

Helen's amused look spoke for her.

"I should be going."

"Wait, Marilyn," Charles said. "I'm not sure you're in the best condition."

"Isn't he a dear?" she said to Helen as she picked up her trench coat and scarf from the floor. "The way he worries." She flung the coat over her shoulder, then cupped Charles' cheek in her hand. "If only more men were like you, Charlie."

Marilyn kissed his cheek and whispered *Bye* to Helen before she left the office.

THE DIOR SUIT had been a point of contention between him and Helen. After opening the box, she had replaced the lid and told Charles to return it. The dress had been one of those gifts he used to give, the kind intended to brighten her and rescue her from the self-inflicted doldrums that kept her in bed, inactive and detached from him and the girls. Such lavish gifts—which included earrings from Tiffany's and Caron Bellodgia perfume—were meant to remind Helen that she'd married a man capable of filling her life with expensive things. She didn't need movie contracts and fame. All he hoped for in return was recognition of his efforts and devotion. Perhaps a whiff of respect.

But the thoughtful presents led nowhere. In fact, Helen remarked, flatly, that she had no use for jewelry and perfume *in the confines of Compton*. After that, Charles lost interest in giving her much of anything.

Now, as she stood before him in his office, he couldn't determine her strategy. Had she worn the dress as a means to disarm him? Was that her way of saying she wanted to save their family? Or was she there to defy him by telling him she was taking the job at the Peacock Lounge?

He waited in silence for her to reveal why she was there. Why she had surprised him, and what her intentions were. Their stare held, and he kept his expression blank, unsure of what he hoped for.

Before the tension between them became unbearable, she said, "Don't bother coming home tonight."

ANGER DIDN'T CONSUME CHARLES, not like he imagined it would when she turned and left him there. Maybe Helen was doing both of them a favor. They needed a break from each other and more so from the suffocating tension trapped under their roof. Although Helen had to be surprised, walking in and finding Marilyn Monroe lounging in her husband's lap, Charles doubted that she believed he was having an affair with the bombshell—no matter what the scene looked like. To that end, Charles didn't think Helen was punishing him. At least not for being with Marilyn.

But Helen's abruptness and decisiveness took him off guard. That was a side of Helen he hardly remembered anymore, and, worthless as the feeling was at the moment, it impressed him. Stirred his long-dead arousal for her.

Charles cleaned up after Helen left. A fog settled over his mind, preventing him from making sense of Helen's visit or Marilyn's session. He put the half-empty bottle of champagne in a refrigerator in the lounge down the hall. The tape recorder sat untouched on the side table. Charles placed it in a drawer with the reel of Marilyn's confessions.

Hunger gnawed at him. He welcomed the change to feel something basic. Instead of Oscar's, he opted for a restaurant down the street. Tucked in a corner table, he paired a Coca-Cola with a tuna fish sandwich and mulled over the possibilities of where he'd spend the night. Bert lived close and didn't have a family to impose upon, but Charles had no desire to explain the situation, which left him with one option. Making the best of a night on the burnt-orange couch.

Back in his office, he telephoned Pam and spoke to the girls. The nervous tick in Judith's voice was apparent when she asked about going home. Soon, Charles promised her. After both girls took turns sharing about their adventures, they gave the receiver back to Pam. Similar to Judith, she asked carefully how things were. Charles avoided specifics but said things with Helen were tenuous. Pam let him leave it at that.

It wasn't as though Charles had never spent a night at his office. Memories of his late-night trysts with the dry cleaner's daughter crept in. As did times when he just didn't want to bear the burden of Helen's depression.

Tonight, even before darkness settled over the city, he dreaded the sleeplessness ahead. Not because of the aches and stiffness the couch was sure to impose, but because he wouldn't be able to get images of Marilyn out of his head. There hadn't been time for him to revel in the delight of having her head in his lap. Looking up at him with those eyes. Her lips stretching into a smile meant only for him.

As he lied on the couch, he couldn't escape wondering where she was spending the night, and with whom. Was she still romanticizing and obsessing over her affair with the president? Still wrapped in the belief they would end up together? For the first time, he dabbled with the unlikely theory that a lack of medication may have heightened her fantasy. Even more unlikely, as her smiling face in his lap ran through his head, he toyed with the idea of her falling in love with him. It wasn't an *impossible* notion.

A knock sounded on the main door to his office and made Charles realize he'd nodded off. The room had grown too dark for him to glimpse the time on the wall clock. He guessed it was nearing midnight. As he rubbed his already throbbing neck, he stumbled to the door and found Bert on the other side.

"What are you doing here?" Charles shielded his eyes from the bright light of the hallway.

"Stopped by your place but it was all quiet." Bert, his Fedora low and tight, stood holding a brown paper bag. "Thought I'd try here. You lose the key to your house or something?"

"Something."

Bert nodded, that smirk of his present.

"Dr. Campbell? Everything all right?"

Both men turned and saw a janitor standing near the end of the hallway, mop in hand.

"Evening, Elliot," Charles said with a wave. "Yes, we're fine. Late night appointment." *One I didn't know about.*

"Should I skip your office, then?"

"Yes, that's fine." Charles opened the office door wider and gave Bert a nod to enter. "Thanks, Elliot. Have a good night."

Charles shut the door as Elliot hesitated, then turned his attention back to the floor.

"Your janitor's got some late hours," Bert said.

"The same could be said for you."

Bert grinned as he set the bag atop the desk in the outer office.

"Dinner is served." Bert pointed to Charles. "You're still a ham and cheese guy, right?"

Charles accepted the food with thanks instead of mentioning that he'd eaten, hours before, and that he hated ham and cheese.

"So after our conversation yesterday, I started poking around, like you wanted. Looks like you got yourself in one hell of a mess."

"Meaning what exactly?"

"This, uh, new client of yours, she's stirring the pot around town, talking about her affair with a certain guy who works in the Oval Office." Bert reached into the bag and pulled out deli wrapped sandwiches and two cans of beer. He tossed the Pabst Blue Ribbon to Charles.

An eerie relief crept over Charles, hearing that someone else knew what Marilyn had told him. But was it wrong, dragging Bert into the situation with him?

"Couple of her so-called friends want her to keep quiet, say she's embarrassing everybody by running her mouth like that. That loverboy of hers has no intention of dumping his pretty wife and shacking up with her."

"My client is a believer in the fairy tale."

"Your client is class-A delusional, and people want her to shut up about her romps with Loverboy, say it's bad for the country, especially with all the heat with Russia. Nobody needs to hear that the world's most powerful guy is more interested in the notches he's carving on his bedpost than the fact that Khrushchev wants to blow this country sky high. So this client of yours might need a lobotomy or a sudden case of amnesia, if you catch my drift."

Charles could smell the baloney from Bert's sandwich. It took him back to their days as roommates, after Bert had ditched Berkley and Charles remained a student. Bert became accustomed to late-night hours and often popped into their apartment when Charles was studying. Arriving with sandwiches in a paper bag became his trademark and made a nice departure from the cans of beans they usually ate.

As much as Charles disliked having to eat the ham and cheese to seem polite, he was more unsettled hearing Marilyn might be in danger. Bert had homed in quickly on Marilyn's antics. Charles could credit it to the fact that Hollywood thrived on gossip, but an itch started in his mind. He recalled Marilyn's concern about someone in her house and her phone being bugged. Speculation sparked within him. Was she was being followed as well? Her every move being monitored since Bert had uncovered information in a short amount of time.

"She needs to remember her place and pipe down." Bert unwrapped his sandwich and took a hearty bite. "Maybe she should work on a movie or go overseas and entertain soldiers again or something."

"Honestly, Bert, I don't know if she's in the frame of mind to do any of those things. She's obsessed with the notion of becoming Mrs. Loverboy."

"Well, according to my sources, there's another problem. She's keeping a diary, possibly filling it with stuff Loverboy and some others have told her. Some of that stuff could affect national security if it got into the wrong hands."

"Hmph. I find that hard to believe. She's not the type who keeps detailed records." *And I can't picture the president rolling over after sex and divulging political secrets.*

"Let me tell you something, Chuck, I'm sure you got a thing for this broad. Who doesn't look at her and want to—"

Charles set his jaw and glared sharply at Bert, warning him not to finish the thought.

"You know what I mean." He put down his sandwich and wiped his mouth.

"I don't like what you're suggesting, Bert. She's my patient."

Bert held up his hands as if surrendering. "Forget it. All I'm trying to do here is help you out. Maybe give you some leverage in the situation. Just hear me out, will ya?"

Charles said nothing but laxed the intensity in his face.

"The way I figure, if you can get close to her, maybe even conduct one or two of your meetings at her house—"

"Why would I do that? I never go to a client's home."

"Tell me if I'm wrong, Chuck, but this gal ain't your run of the mill client."

Charles didn't argue. In fact, he pictured Marilyn at Greenson's home, having breakfast, then swimming in his pool.

"As I was saying, you cozy up to her somehow, get an invite to her place, and you look for that diary. Find that book, and if something goes sideways with this gal, you're covered."

Self-preservation. Exactly how Charles and Bert survived and navigated growing up in New Jersey. *Look out for yourself by any means necessary*, had been a piece of advice Bert's father had drilled into them when they were young. Working as a private investigator, Bert probably regarded ethical conduct as a suggestion, and if Charles had to guess, his pal ended up in his fair share of scrapes. All in the name of self-preservation.

Such tactics worked for Bert, and had for Charles long ago, when he was a different kind of man. Now, Charles had a professional reputation to uphold. Snooping in a client's private space and possibly stealing from her weren't options.

Charles sat on the edge of his desk. "I haven't had much luck with her so far. She's erratic during our sessions, and I suspect she's taking too many pills."

"I heard that people might get rough with her. Loverboy has made some unsavory friends, and his old man pulled a lot of strings to get him set up in Washington. She needs to get her act together."

Charles thought of the bruises on Marilyn. Had someone already threatened her and given her a taste of what could happen? Seemed unlikely, since she didn't appear shaken, but this was a woman who nonchalantly mentioned Hoover might be bugging her house.

"Sounds like Loverboy's biggest concern is some hot shot reporter getting wind of their affair. It's speculation right now, but the birthday event amped up curiosities. He's got most of those saps in his pockets, though, protecting his image, cause from what I hear, he's been chasing skirts all his life. You wouldn't believe all the women who fall for that horse-tooth smile."

Charles believed it. The public couldn't get enough of Kennedy and his family. They exuded youth and patriotism and new ideas.

"My client thinks she's on the verge of becoming first lady before his first term is up. Are you telling me she's not special to him?"

Bert returned to his sandwich. "He got what he wanted in Palm Springs, and I don't know what she's telling you, but that's the only time he's been alone with her, which is why it's a mess. She's trying to turn it into something it ain't."

Not the impression Charles had. He stewed inwardly, wondering why Marilyn had been set to play him for a fool.

"I'm glad I ain't you." Bert churned a bite of sandwich in his mouth.

"Why's that?"

"Are you kiddin' me? With all the heat she's creating, Loverboy might have someone shut her down. Wouldn't surprise me if they wanted to check out who she's been talking to in case they got any *loose ends* that need takin' care of. Because you know he's plannin' on winnin' another four years. Matter of fact, wouldn't surprise me if we ended up with a Kennedy in the White House for the next decade or more. A real dynasty. And they ain't lettin' nothin' get in the way. Especially no broad. No, I don't want no Feds knocking down my door, asking me what I know. You'll be on some sort of hot list soon, pal, if you aren't already."

FIVE

Charles knew better than to inquire how Bert culled his information. Even so, instinct told him what Bert had shared probably rang true—with the glaring fact that Marilyn was in trouble.

Talk about Hoover, phones being bugged, and thugs on his heels had him spooked. He abandoned the plan to sleep at his office. After Bert left, and Charles passed on the offer to stay at Bert's, he grabbed a couple items and drove to Long Beach.

Good fortune prevailed, and he obtained a room, late as it was, at the Golden Sails Hotel. Not so long ago, the place had been his favorite getaway spot with Helen and the girls. Memorable weekends were spent picnicking on the beach, sunbathing, and splashing in the ocean. With seagulls serenading and sand melting between his toes, Charles thought life was perfect. He even wanted more children and told Helen so. But she withdrew from him and soon lost interest in their weekend beach retreats.

Once he was in the room, memories abundant and painful flooded his mind. He telephoned home, mindless of the late hour. When Helen didn't answer he wasn't surprised. He also wasn't going to bother toying with the possibilities of why she didn't pick up.

For the remainder of the night, his companion would be the meaty file Bill Stewart had placed in his hands little more than a week ago. Charles had picked it up before leaving his office and was convinced it deserved another once-over. The more he read and reread Marilyn's medical history, though, the more riled he became about her use of chlordiazepoxide, Nembutal, and generic barbiturates.

Along with lists of medications and hospital stays, the file contained various test shots of the actress in her films. Charles had a soft spot for *The Prince and the Showgirl*. Maybe it reminded him of Helen and the way he'd plucked her from that hard-knock-life of showbiz. He'd swept her off her feet, as any prince would. Treated her to late night dinners, gifts and flowers, and walks along the Santa Monica Pier that often ended with watching the sunrise.

Once upon a time, her impulsiveness had pleased him.

Exhaustion began to set in, and he would need to resolve issues with Helen later. He refocused on the file. In particular, he wanted to find Marilyn's address and telephone number. Not being able to connect with her apart from their sessions was in adequate. But after flipping through the pages again, he discovered no information. It also occurred to him that he had no telephone number for Bill Stewart, either.

Even though his own experience with Marilyn had been unproductive and frustrating, Charles wasn't ready to give up on her. She needed him, more than ever. That superseded his concerns about whether or not she had played him.

He disagreed with Bert's assessment about leverage. As far as he was concerned, there was no leverage. Because if word got out, as it often did in Hollywood, that Charles had the recording of Marilyn casually spilling details about her dalliances with Kennedy, wouldn't Hoover or the president unleash thugs upon him? Same with finding Marilyn's diary. Such items were liabilities.

Charles closed the file and stretched out on the duvet cover that smelled like the beach. Going forward, he planned to communicate better with Marilyn and prove to her that his only agenda was to safeguard her wellbeing.

THE SHOWER FELT pointless the next morning when Charles put his clothes back on from the day before, but he had no choice. Had he been in a better mind frame, and if the coffee he picked up on his way to the office had been stronger, he would've cared more about that untidy feel.

Charles went through the usual motions as morning patients came and went, but he wasn't fully present. Marital woes bogged him down. So did his concern for Marilyn. He missed the illusion of control and stability his life once projected.

His mental listlessness took a turn when Marilyn didn't arrive for her session. Dread moved in and took its place. Having no way to get in touch and check on her, helplessness plagued him.

"DADDY! DADDY!" Judith and Natalie squealed when Charles pulled into Jim and Pam's driveway later that Friday afternoon.

Before locking up and leaving the office, he had called Pam. Although nothing had been resolved with Helen, he could have used more time alone but didn't want to take advantage of Pam's generosity. Plus, he missed his little ones more than expected.

The girls greeted him on the lawn when he got out of the car. Kisses and neck squeezes were in abundance. The girls climbed into the Buick and started waving good-bye to their aunt.

"Problems solved already?" Pam held out the girls' suitcase.

"A temporary truce." Lying, he decided, was better than explaining. Not that there was much he could explanation, even if he had the strength. "Thanks, Pam, thanks for everything." Charles kissed her on the cheek.

He joined the girls and eased out of the driveway. A measure of gratefulness struck him, knowing his girls were too young to see through his ploy, unlike Pam, who stood waving, her face expressionless and unbelieving.

DURING THE RIDE HOME, Charles told the girls he had an idea.

"When we get there, let's go up and ring the doorbell. Mommy will be so surprised."

The girls laughed and said it would be fun. When they arrived, twilight began to mute the sky, and doubt ramped in Charles as he worried over whether he'd made the right move. Natalie pushed the button with her little finger, and the melody of the chime meant there was no turning back.

Truthfully, he didn't want to face Helen alone. Didn't want the laborious work of cajoling her into an even temper. Having the girls at his side was a sure way back into the house, without an altercation. Or so he hoped.

When Helen opened the front door, it was clear to Charles that she had switched into the role of delighted mother. She knelt, welcomed the girls into her arms and dramatized how she'd missed them. Charles knew better but went along. He recognized that dark spot in Helen's eyes, where resentment lived.

He was counting on her being unable to turn them away as they stood there on the front porch of their family home while Mrs. Gibson watched from next door, Hercules the cat curled in her lap. Helen stood back and let them in. Charles tossed a wave and a *Good evening* to Mrs. Gibson, who did little more than grunt in return. He found her icy stare more welcoming than the tension awaiting him inside.

"WELL, girls, you are going to be so proud of your Mommy." Helen sat after serving up the reheated remains, Charles assumed, of a casserole found in the back of the refrigerator.

Charles poked it with his fork. If he remembered correctly, it wasn't a favorite the first time around. But it gave him something to do instead of obsessing over the smallness of things, like the heavy aroma of Pine-Sol, which Helen only touched when she was angry, and the fact that Helen was making a point of ignoring him and speaking only to the girls.

"What?" Judith asked, bright eyed.

Natalie hardly looked up. Charles knew, from her shriveled-up posture, she dreaded the casserole more than he did.

"I got the part!"

Charles gave her a blank stare while the girls kept quiet.

"I got the lead in the play, in Culver City! Rehearsals start next week. And a few nights a week, I'll be singing at The Peacock Lounge! Isn't that wonderful?"

"What's wonderful about it?" Natalie asked.

Helen hesitated. "It's wonderful because I'm an actress. Soon I'll be in movies, and won't you enjoy telling everyone that your mommy is a famous star?"

"Who will we tell?" Judith asked.

"Everyone."

"Even Mrs. Gibson?" Natalie was among the few who braved Mrs. Gibson's doorstep and ventured inside on occasion. Only a handful of neighbors received such hospitality from the widow and her cat.

"Yes, of course."

"She doesn't like movies."

Helen said nothing.

"Mommy, don't you go have to go away to make movies?" Judith said.

"Sometimes—"

"Then it's not wonderful," Natalie added.

Tears glistened in Helen's eyes. Charles wondered if it was from the frustration of the girls not understanding the so-called prestige that came with being a famous Hollywood actress. Or if it was from the girls stealing the joy of her moment—her moment of putting Charles in his place and telling him how life would soon be.

Either way, he had no desire to make things easier on her.

"Congratulations, Helen." He tossed his fork onto the plate and gave up the half-hearted charade.

Helen sprang from her seat and ran back to her bedroom. A slamming door sounded.

"Why does Mommy want to be in movies?" Natalie asked.

"Mommy wants to be famous and wants everyone to know her name."

Charles couldn't help the harsh tone. His acting skills lacked finesse. But what did it matter anymore? When did life stop being about Helen and her degree of discontent? He sighed, attempting to calm his aggravation. The girls didn't deserve his anger.

He went into the kitchen and pulled open the freezer. Two Swanson TV dinners awaited. Charles took them out and looked to the girls.

"We could share," he said.

Judith and Natalie traded glances.

Charles knew they had few choices, and not just when it came to their dinner. He knew Helen was determined to make what life they had miserable because she was miserable. Charles was done tolerating it. He would make the best of the situation, including dinner. And when Natalie only ate the pie, he wouldn't complain.

"Tell you what," he said, "you two can each have the Dutch apple pie."

Relief hit him when their shy smiles appeared. They were buoyed even more when they scraped the casserole remains from their plates and into the wastebasket.

When Charles went to pre-heat the oven, he caught a glimpse of the calendar, hanging in the kitchen. Dread struck him like a wrecking ball. Tomorrow had BBQ written in bold letters. Naturally, he'd forgotten. Helen would remember though, she always did. She'd punish him, the way she always did, with the whole neighborhood watching.

WHEN IT CAME to the summer succession of barbeques the neighbors held, Charles believed he deserved an Academy Award for each performance. It wasn't that he didn't like the people in his tight-knit community; he didn't like the show Helen insisted upon. For years now, the gatherings had been her only audience, and she never failed them, especially when it was their turn to host.

Such as today.

Now, he understood why the house had smelled of an angry scrub down, why the rubber gloves had been folded over the kitchen sink last night, and why Helen had made little fuss about his return with the girls. It was all about today. Nothing, not even catching her husband with Marilyn Monroe in his lap, would spoil her Saturday afternoon in the neighborhood spotlight.

A saving grace for Charles was that he didn't have to think. Routine, combined with a sliver of expectation, took over. He wore the clothes folded and waiting on his valet chair, then readied the grill and set up the backyard. Helen focused on the girls, braiding ribbons in their hair and making sure their dresses were perfect.

Neighbors trickled in through the side gate, bearing gifts of casseroles and desserts. Charles kept his post at the barbeque until Niles Griffith arrived. Discretely, Charles squared up with him over the grocery bill the girls had charged, and he thanked him for handling the matter with such kindness and sensitivity.

Without much sympathy, Mr. Griffith nodded. "There's always been something wrong with that wife of yours, Campbell. Being a doctor, you should be able to manage your family better." He moved into the crowd, uninterested in Charles' reply.

Charles didn't have a chance to dwell on Mr. Griffith's remark, as neighbors Ted and Al joined him, with beers in hand, at the barbeque.

"Hot one today." Al wiped the back of his neck with a handkerchief. Few would guess that during business hours Al managed the State Savings Bank downtown. On weekends and at social gatherings, he swapped his neatly pressed dress shirts for Hawaiian shirts, unbuttoned and exposing his undershirt.

"Always is," Ted replied. In contrast to Al, Ted preferred chinos and a shirt, much like Charles. Taller, leaner than Al or Charles, Ted enjoyed being mistaken for George Reeves on occasion, and he had a grating habit of making sure he was the first on the block with the latest appliance, kitchen gadget, or television model. Perks of being a divorce lawyer, he once boasted.

"Did you listen to the Dodger game last night?" Ted asked.

"Lookin' good this year," Al said.

Charles paid little attention. Usually, seeing Al and Ted meant a reprieve from work and Helen's extremes. Even though Ted's and Al's at-home roles and responsibilities were different than his. From the way they talked about their wives and kids, Charles knew neither of them got up in the middle of the night to change sheets if a child was sick or wet the bed. They didn't play paper dolls with their girls, and they didn't make their own TV dinners. Despite their complaints that their wives shunned them in bed on occasion, they were respected in their homes.

But now, Charles had a secret. He'd been spending afternoons with Marilyn Monroe. Ted and Al, he knew, would both give their right arms to be in the same room with her. Charles figured they wouldn't believe him anyway, especially when it came to the part about Marilyn with her head in his lap, sharing a bottle of champagne. He grinned, thinking on it.

"I see Helen's keepin' that smile on your face," Al said.

"You are one lucky pork chop, my friend." Ted slightly backhanded Charles in the gut.

Both men looked Helen's way. As usual, she was stunning and over-dressed for a backyard gathering. Charles suspected Helen had a girdle on, enhancing her slim waist and pleasing cleavage. But how would he know? He couldn't recall the last time he'd made love with his wife or seen her naked. He sipped root beer through gritted teeth and gave a play-along nod.

Ted shook his head. "Doesn't get much finer than her."

Charles had to give Helen credit. She had planted the perception that she was a vixen, an adoring wife, and a good mother.

He could educate Ted and Al, air his marital problems as they finished their beers and ate their hamburgers. But baring the truth about Helen would only reflect badly on him. Mr. Griffith had made that clear.

Charles stuck with grilling the hamburgers. For a moment, he wondered if all their conversations were this dull, revolving around the Dodgers, the last time they'd had their cars lubed. But what would interest Charles these days? Talking about Marilyn? He'd enjoy the jeal-ousy sure to paint their faces, but what did it mean? If Ted and Al heard the details of his unorthodox sessions with Marilyn, was there anything for them to be jealous about? It wasn't as though she found Charles irresistible. There was no danger of her becoming infatuated, falling in love with him. Was there? After all, what could he mean—what did he mean—to Marilyn? It hurt his head thinking on it. He stuck with searing the hamburgers against the grill.

THE CHARCOAL SMOLDERED as the sunset kissed the horizon. Abandoned disposable plates flickered in the light breeze while cups lay overturned, rolling in their spills. Remnants of a decent party, Charles thought. He grabbed the aluminum trash can from the side of the garage and began cleaning up. Helen, who seemed pleased with the day, had taken the girls in for a bath.

If he were Ted or Al, Charles could feel good about the day and how it played out. But satisfaction eluded him. He knew when he walked back into that house, the role playing would be dead. Helen's performance was over, and their problems would be waiting. What would he say to her now that she'd gotten her way with both the play and the singing gig? She had defied him. For Charles, it was close to a final straw and proved to him that she cared nothing about their marriage. Or about what he needed and expected as a husband.

How would he face her?

"Psst!"

Charles whipped his head toward the bushes lining the side of the house and saw a hunched figure, cloaked in a headscarf and wearing dark sunglasses.

"Charlie, it's me, Marilyn," she said in a whisper.

Charles set down the trash can and went to her.

"I hate to bother you." She slipped off the sunglasses. "I saw your party."

"No, no, it's fine," Charles said. Seeing her there erased his discontent. "What are you doing here?"

"Well, I wanted to see you."

Her voice, breathy and gentle, smoothed over him like warm hands against bare skin. The sensation left him speechless.

"I was wondering...." She hesitated and bit her lower lip. "Could you give me a ride home?"

"Now?"

She nodded.

Confusion and a mild sense of aggravation wrestled inside him. Mixed with his rising body heat. He didn't waste time sorting it.

Charles darted a glance to the patio door. "Just give me a minute."

He rushed inside and desperately hoped Helen was still occupied with the girls. He snatched the car keys and his wallet. At the sight of his wedding ring on his finger, he made a fist. Was there a chance Marilyn hadn't noticed it? Charles removed it, dropped it in a drawer. He considered leaving a note for Helen but decided it wasn't worth the risk of getting caught in the backyard with Marilyn.

―――――――――

IN THE CAR, Marilyn became a firecracker of conversation. She removed her headscarf and primped her hair in the rearview mirror. With her bare shoulder touching Charles, she gave him directions back to her place. She was also pleased with herself, she said, taking a taxi and finding Charles' home all on her own.

His emotions continued to churn, a side effect of being near Marilyn. One he wasn't accustomed to. Undeniable excitement entwined with skepticism. Was he really about to be alone with Marilyn Monroe ―a client―at her Brentwood home? Perhaps she needed him. What if there was a situation that only Charles could fix for her? That only he could be trusted to handle―not Greenson or anyone else.

No. He shoved the ridiculous notions away. What was he thinking? He was nothing more than a chump, playing into her hands, believing that he had an ounce of control in this dream called Marilyn.

He figured she must have found his address from the telephone book. Easy enough. He wanted to ask why she missed her appointment yesterday, but he had a feeling it didn't matter. Being next to her and experiencing her vivaciousness were all he cared about.

When they pulled into the driveway at 12305 Fifth Helena Drive, Charles felt his knees quiver. Whether it was an overdose of adrenaline or a mounting fear that he was suddenly being watched he couldn't say.

Marilyn came to his side of the car and took him by the arm as she led him inside. Charles' unease shifted to astonishment when he crossed the threshold. Scantily furnished and with barren walls, the home of the world's most famous female starlet looked vacant and barely lived in. He expected bear rugs, chandeliers dripping with crystals, maybe even movie posters or a full bar and a grand piano. Instead, he walked into a plain white space, void of personality and lacking identity.

Taking it in, Charles was introduced to Eunice Murray, Marilyn's housekeeper.

"Such a pleasure meeting you, doctor." Warmth and sincerity emanated from Eunice's smile and gentle handshake. "Marilyn's told me a great deal about you and how wonderful you've been for her."

"Has she?" Three sessions had catapulted Charles Campbell to the status of wonderful? What was there for Marilyn to share about him? That he allowed her to bounce around his office like an unruly child? Or that she flirted and toyed with him yet he managed to keep his hands to himself? Not that it mattered.

More important was meeting someone who knew Marilyn personally. Someone who had insights. If a chance presented itself, Charles thought he might be able to discover more about Marilyn through talking to Eunice. Privately, of course.

"I'll see about a little something for dinner."

"Oh, don't bother, Eunie," Marilyn said. "We're really not hungry. You can head home for the night. I'm sure Charlie will take care of me." She giggled.

"All right, dear. As long as you're in good hands." Eunice patted Charles on his arm and gave him an approving smile.

Charles felt limp with bewilderment. Eunice gathered her purse and shuffled out the back door.

So much for chatting with Eunice.

Turning to Marilyn, Charles saw she was drinking straight from a bottle of Dom Perignon. Again.

"Are you sure that's a good idea?" Charles hated her fondness for alcohol. Almost as much as he hated sounding like a pestering chaperone.

"Don't worry, Charlie. A few little drinks will help me relax."

Flashbacks of his father struck him. The drunken demon, roused and angry, exploding its fury on his mother. Charles blinked hard to chase the images away.

What would it do to Marilyn? Make her angry? Even more sultry?

Charles considered leaving. She was home, thanks to him. Safe with no emergency present. Nothing good could come from watching her get drunk, he was certain.

Marilyn came up to him and held the bottle just beneath his lips.

"Want some?" Her eyes had that innocent sparkle, and a playful invitation lingered.

His pulse ramped up, and the surging made thinking straight difficult. He could wrap his arms around her, right then, pull her into him and let pleasure have its way. Toss every scrap of professional and personal ethics to the wind.

"Why am I here, Marilyn?"

"Isn't it obvious?"

Charles waited.

"I didn't want to be alone." She touched her fingertip to his cheek then traced his jawline.

"You came to my house. I thought there was an emergency—"

"You're angry with me."

"No, I'm just trying to understand. Marilyn, please, I'm worried about you and want to help you."

She turned away from him and took a swig from the bottle.

"That's what everyone says. They all want to *help me*." She said it with a firm tone Charles hadn't heard from her before. "Why is it that everyone else seems to know what's best for me? I'm a grown woman, capable of taking care of myself."

Charles didn't know what to say.

"You're talking like a doctor, Charlie. It's boring. I thought you wanted us to be friends."

"Of course! But your behavior, Marilyn, and all the pills. It concerns me." This wasn't how Charles envisioned approaching the topics with her, but what other way was there to reach this woman? Her fleeting attention span exasperated him.

"Can't we just enjoy each other's company? I don't want to talk about anything really." She took another swill from the bottle.

"Marilyn—"

"I know! Let's go for a swim! It's such a beautiful night." She reached behind her neck and tugged on the zipper of her dress. A few maneuvers and she peeled the dress from her body like she was removing a second skin. Charles stood paralyzed as her intimates slipped to the floor. Perhaps he was no gentleman, not in the truest sense of the word, but he averted his eyes and tried to catch his breath.

"Come on, Charlie! Don't be shy."

He heard the soles of her feet slap the tile and scamper outside to the pool. Sounds of splashing and delighted squeals drifted into the house.

Charles sank onto the edge of a sofa. He dropped his face into his hands and tried to slow the thoughts racing through his head. The longing for physical touch and the fulfillment of being with a woman began to rage inside him. He clenched the cushions and gritted his teeth. How had he ended up here? Not just at Marilyn Monroe's house, but on the cusp of having another affair. He learned from the first time that carnal pleasures didn't last or heal a broken marriage. That momentary bliss never outlasted the pangs of guilt.

He'd been convinced he could live with that guilt. Until he found himself sitting across from Helen at the dinner table, lying about his day and what he'd done. He'd sat on the floor, playing with his girls, as though he still deserved their adoration and their perfect love. Ironically, he discovered, the temporary satisfaction he found meant nothing when he realized how it compromised him. At the very least, his daughters needed—deserved—a father with integrity.

Helen's behavior couldn't be his excuse.

Another reason he'd ended the affair.

Even though his marriage was in greater shambles now than during his indiscretion, he couldn't do it. As much as the carnal beast within him craved sex with her, Charles couldn't take advantage of Marilyn like that. He couldn't use her for his own gratification or for revenge toward Helen.

Plus, Marilyn had to be acting out of character. She had to be racked from pills and alcohol. Otherwise, was he to believe she simply wanted his company? That, hardly knowing him, she wanted to be alone with him *and* go skinny dipping? Clearly, behavior-altering substances had to be involved.

He moved from the sofa to the patio doors and glimpsed Marilyn out in the pool. The dimming light and water blurred her nude body as she swam proficiently. All he had to do was shed his clothes and join her. She was his for the taking. But he kept to the inside of the threshold and wondered what was wrong with him.

HE DECLINED her invitation to join her, much as it pained him as a man.

"I'll get you some towels." He went back inside the house, convinced that putting more distance between them was the only defense he had. Resisting the temptation was clawing him from the inside. What would he do when she came out of the water and was naked in front of him? The pictures inside LIFE magazine flashed through his mind. Knowing how those photos excited him, well, he gave serious thought to leaving altogether.

He found a linen closet with fresh towels and took a couple. Before he shut the door, he recalled what Bert had said about Marilyn keeping a diary. A record of her secrets and information that perhaps Hoover and Kennedy both wanted to get their hands on. Charles felt his way through the closet's items but came up empty. Instant shame jolted him, but snooping would help keep his mind off Marilyn.

Maybe Bert was right. If he found the diary, and it was chocked full of revelations, it might safeguard him. He could warn any Feds or goons that showed up on his doorstep, that he would make sure the diary reached the *L.A. Times* and *San Francisco Chronicle*, if anything happened to Marilyn. Or to him and his family. He didn't know if he had the backbone needed to play such a game, or if the threat was as potent as he hoped, but he decided to search for the diary anyway—and ignore the absurdity of it all.

Charles focused on areas where Marilyn might hide it. He started with the desk in the living room. Scripts littered the desktop and were marred with dog-eared pages and notations in red ink. An assortment of photos of Marilyn with Joe DiMaggio also occupied space. Drawers held more pictures, including snapshots of Marilyn with Marlon Brando and Clark Gable. Bank statements surfaced, bewildering Charles with their paltry amounts. He sifted through the debris, noting how the mess commented on Marilyn's fragmented life. But no diary.

Cautious of his every move, he went into the kitchen and glimpsed into every drawer and mostly bare cabinets. He patted the top of the refrigerator, finding only dust.

He moved to the bedroom. A heightened tension grabbed him as he knew he was invading her most private area for his own selfish motives. He rummaged through her closet only slightly, then plunged his fingers under the mattress on her unmade bed. Pill bottles on Marilyn's nightstand derailed his search.

Charles went to them and examined the labels. Greenson's name appeared on two of the bottles. Three more bottles displayed different pharmacies but mentioned no doctors. Librium. Percodan. Valmid. Chloral Hydrate. Nembutal. No one, he concluded, needed such a quantity of prescriptions—especially the sedatives. But an eerie panic erupted in Charles when he realized all of the bottles were empty.

CHARLES DARTED TO THE POOL, but the rippling waters were quiet. Marilyn was gone. He scanned the backyard and found her on a lounge chair, robed and lying still with her eyes closed. The robe, he figured, must've already been there. It clung to her wet body like seaweed.

"Marilyn!"

He touched her shoulder, but she didn't move. How long he'd been in the house snooping, he couldn't say. Just as he had no idea how long she'd been there. Unconscious.

Charles checked her pulse. Weak and thready beats met his fingertips.

He ran into the house and dialed the Operator. Frantically, he told her to send an ambulance and gave the address.

Charles returned to Marilyn.

Had she taken the pills from the bottles in the bedroom? Fear hit him like a lightning strike. Was he too late? And was this a set up? Was Marilyn Monroe staging her suicide with Dr. Charles Campbell at her side?

SIX

Paramedics arrived within minutes, and Charles was grateful that reporters were not in tow. If news leaked out that Marilyn Monroe was lying unconscious poolside, he knew they would gather like vultures.

"She might've overdosed on pills." Charles handed them the bottles he brought from her bedroom.

A mild dose of adrenaline was administered.

Marilyn gasped and slowly roused.

"Marilyn, Marilyn, can you hear me?" Charles nudged aside a paramedic.

Her gaze slowly slid across the faces before her. When she found Charles, a slight smile appeared.

"Charlie...." She reached a hand toward him. He responded by taking her hand into both of his.

"Did you take the pills, Marilyn?"

"...Pills...?"

He showed her an empty bottle.

"These. Did you swallow all of these?"

She gave a weak laugh and shook her head.

Confused, Charles said, "But the bottles are empty. Five bottles of pills."

"Down the commode," Marilyn said through her laugh.

Charles glanced at the paramedics, who shared his puzzlement, then focused again on Marilyn. "I don't understand."

"No more pills for me." She swiped her other hand as though she was pushing the pill bottles away. "I sent them all away."

"Sir, please," said a paramedic. "You need to step back and let us work."

Charles nodded and moved back.

"We should get her to Cedars," said the other paramedic.

"No!" Marilyn said, half sitting up. "No hospital. No hospital."

Charles knew why. Not only was she terrified of hospitals since the Payne Whitney incident, but her mother had spent most of her life in and out of sanitariums with little to no improvement of her mental state.

"It's fine, Marilyn. There won't be any hospitals."

The paramedics looked miffed but concentrated on tending to Marilyn rather than arguing. Charles paced beside the pool while they took her vitals. He cursed Dr. Ralph Greenson under his breath and prayed that Marilyn was telling the truth about the pills.

———

DEHYDRATION AND EXHAUSTION were blamed for Marilyn's loss of consciousness. The paramedics advised her to follow up with her doctor as soon as possible. She flashed a smile at Charles. Plenty of rest and a decent meal were also recommended before the paramedics departed.

Charles breathed easier as color reappeared in Marilyn's cheeks. Since she couldn't remember the last time she'd eaten, Charles revisited the kitchen cabinets and returned with a jelly bread and a glass of orange juice. Not a meal by any means but something for her stomach. If he had the chance, he'd ask Marilyn what Eunice did around the house. Empty cabinets and a bare refrigerator indicated that the so-called housekeeper didn't do much.

"I must look like a drenched rat." Marilyn ran her hand over her damp hair. Charles had covered her with towels and insisted that she relax while he fixed her sandwich.

"We'd better get you in some dry clothes." He helped her to her feet and held her close as he led her to her room. "Should I call Eunice or anyone?"

"No. I'm glad you're here, Charlie. I don't need anyone else."

Her words made him feel warm and nauseous at the same time.

"Are you sure? You really shouldn't be alone tonight."

"Does that mean you're leaving me?" Distress tinged her voice.

Charles hesitated. He'd been gone for hours and sent no word home. The girls were in bed by now, he hoped, but Helen was surely fuming. Or at least mystified by his disappearance.

"I—I want to do whatever makes you comfortable."

"Then stay."

He didn't know the right decision.

"You're the only person I want to be with me." Her remark complicated his ability to reason. With the arm she had draped around his shoulders, she squeezed him closer. The scent of chlorine on her skin stung his nose but reminded him of her in the pool—in the magazine pictures—naked and vulnerable. She nuzzled against his neck and whispered his name.

"I'll stay, Marilyn. I'll stay."

———

CHARLES PICKED up a bagful of groceries at a corner store while Marilyn showered. Not knowing what she liked, he stuck with the basic staples and a surplus of fruit. He stared at a payphone as he cruised past. There was no explaining this to Helen over the telephone.

Carrying the groceries into Marilyn's house, he felt an odd pang of domestic bliss, if he could call it that. Here he was, walking in on someone who'd be genuinely happy to see him. Someone he'd known merely days. And truth be told, he had no business being at this particular someone's home.

Yet there he was. Groceries in hand. A smile on his face.

But his special someone didn't greet him the way he imagined she would. Darkness filled much of the house. Charles knew that knot of dread that formed in his stomach all too well.

"Marilyn?"

No answer came, but he found Marilyn in her bedroom. Smoking and talking on the phone, she wore a lacy negligee that was perfect for *Some Like it Hot*—or for greeting her lover.

Charles reddened.

Was she expecting a lover? What in God's name would Charles do if the president made his way through the front door?

"I'll just be a minute," Marilyn said with her hand covering the receiver.

Charles nodded and retreated to the kitchen. Redeeming himself from the jelly bread sandwich, he whipped up a small bowl of oatmeal and a glass of warm milk.

Returning to Marilyn's bedroom with a small tray, Charles heard her bid good-bye to the party on the other end of the telephone.

"I know it's not much," he said, "and it's not the gourmet cuisine you're probably used to." He glimpsed the half-empty bottle of champagne on Marilyn's nightstand and moved it to the floor as he slid the small tray into its place.

She slouched. "You are the sweetest man! Thank you, but I'm really just tired."

"Oh, then I should—"

"Would you stay with me? Please?" She took his hand and began to caress his skin gently with her thumb.

His breath caught. "I shouldn't. I mean, I'm sure there's someone else you'd rather be with." Projecting a whiny and insecure persona, Charles didn't recognize himself. Embarrassment inadequately described the roil in his chest.

"Don't be silly, Charlie." She scooted over and pulled Charles onto the bed. He sat, stiff and straight and on the edge of the mattress. She fluffed the pillow beside her, patted it for him to lie down next to her, but Charles didn't dare.

"There's nothing worse than being alone." She fell back onto her pillow. "I can't stand being alone." She paused a moment, then shrugged. "Maybe it's this house. I'm still not used to it."

Or maybe it's the fact that you might be under surveillance.

Marilyn rolled onto her side. "Would you do a great big favor for me, Charlie?"

With his pulse at full throttle, he almost couldn't speak. "Sure."

"There's a hairbrush on the floor by the bed. Could you brush my hair until I fall asleep? Please?"

Charles found the brush and turned sideways. As he leaned toward her with the brush extended, his hand quivered. Despite his nervousness, he began stroking her hair with a gentle ease. The trembling subsided. And Marilyn groaned her satisfaction.

"So relaxing," she said, her voice softly fading.

"Are you sure you're all right, Marilyn? You gave me quite a scare earlier."

"Don't fret, Charlie. I'm fine."

"And you're certain you didn't take any of those pills?"

"No more pills for me."

"Oh." Charles bristled. "Was that Greenson's idea?"

She laughed, carefree and with a lilt in her tone.

"No. I decided, because I know it might not be good for the baby."

Baby?

Charles stopped brushing.

"Are you telling me that you're pregnant, Marilyn?"

"Mmm-hmm." She cuddled into her pillow with her cheek. "That's why I'm so dangerous."

CHARLES FELT STUPID. He waited until Marilyn was asleep before leaving the bed and sitting in the hallway. With his back against the wall, he hated that he'd asked Marilyn if she was pregnant. Wasn't she concerned that her house had been bugged, that someone was listening in? If that were true—and Charles had a sinking feeling that it was—then someone knew he was in her house—and that she'd confessed to being pregnant. Surely, Charles thought, the powers that be weren't going to sit back while Marilyn, erratic and unpredictable, was armed with a damaging secret. And what did that mean for him? What would it mean for Marilyn?

Was any of this real?

Was he really there, inside Marilyn Monroe's house, droopy-eyed and sitting in her hallway, reeling over the repercussions the country would face when news broke that she was pregnant—presumably—with President Kennedy's baby?

EXHAUSTION TOOK HOLD, and Charles drifted into a busy sleep. In the dead of night, the blaring ring of the telephone rattled him. He'd forgotten where he was, but the carpet against his cheek and the strangeness surrounding him reminded him he was in Marilyn's house. On his hands and knees, he crawled into her room toward the obnoxious blast.

Marilyn didn't stir.

Charles tumbled the receiver off its cradle, relieved to end the trumpeting, and held the phone to his ear. His mouth was too dry to form words.

"I know you're there, doll," said a man's voice, his East coast accent apparent to Charles. "You all doped up on them pills again? Huh?"

Charles said nothing.

"They wanted me to call you," the man continued. "They said you're gettin' outta hand, Marilyn. Look, I know it ain't all your fault, baby, but they're right. People are talkin', gettin' edgy. You need to lay low a couple weeks." His voice deepened. "And I gotta be honest here. If you ain't careful, well...they ain't gonna be nice about it. You get what I'm sayin'? You gotta accept that it's over. Stop calling him. He's done with you. I tried warning you, tellin' you he's a waste of time. He's like that, you know."

Charles looked to Marilyn's sleeping silhouette. When he imagined what hearing those words would do to her, he cringed inwardly.

"It ain't what you wanna hear, but the foolin' around is over. You should just forget all this mess and let me take care of you. Maybe come out here to the lodge with me and the fellas for a while. I'll take care of you, baby. We never gave things a fair shot between us. Maybe it's time, Marilyn." Silence hung, then, "I'll be out there soon. We can talk about it later. Sleep on it, okay?"

With that, Charles heard the line disconnect.

———

KNOWING SLEEP WAS IMPOSSIBLE, Charles kept a vigil over Marilyn for the last fleeting hours of night. He peeked out every window but saw no one. Then he resumed his search for the diary. Even after double-checking areas he'd already been to, he came up empty-handed. He didn't turn on lights and had to rely on soft streams of moonlight that filtered in. Hunting for listening devices, as well as the diary, he patted down lamps and ran his hands along the furniture, like he'd seen in movies. The search produced nothing.

Desperate for fresh air and a chance to clear his head, he parked himself outside on the lounge chair near the pool. A feeble attempt at retaining a sliver of decency in the situation, he thought. Watching the sunrise paint the early morning sky gave him a false sense of hope.

Part of him regretted not calling Helen or leaving a note. Not because he felt a sudden concern toward her feelings, but he dreaded the effort of explanation, of getting back into the house. But that was what they did. Capitalize on hurting each other. Charles didn't know another way at this point, but he wanted to create a better life for Judith and Natalie. Even if it meant divorcing Helen.

"Morning, sleepy head," Marilyn said behind him. The sunlight seemed dull next to her radiance, and Charles was amazed at what sleep had done for her.

He knew he had to be an eyesore.

"You look refreshed." He ignored the aches in his neck and shoulders from sleeping in the hallway.

"Can I make you breakfast?" she asked.

"That's sweet of you, but I should be going."

"Oh, please, let me! It would be my way of thanking you for staying."

She was frustrating, Charles had to admit. When he pulled back, she intentionally drew him in. But she retracted when the conversation wasn't to her liking. Perhaps gaining her trust would be his demise. Retreat seemed his best option.

"Eggs and toast?" he asked.

"Perfect!" She clapped before twirling around and heading to the kitchen.

Charles no longer knew who he was in Marilyn's presence. Scatter-brained and reckless best defined him. Most annoying was the way he allowed Marilyn to manipulate him. He tolerated her antics and fed her delusions as if he were no better than a marionette on strings. More pathetic than a man hiding his wedding ring, he had become a willing victim of her charms and rapturous beauty.

He settled at the kitchen table and watched her flit from cabinets to stove to refrigerator like a bird trapped in a glass cage. Lucky, he thought, that he'd picked up groceries at the store yesterday. Not that Marilyn noticed or made mention of it.

"When did you find out about the baby?" Maybe he was a cad for starting off the morning by sounding insensitive. Crude sleep and the strangeness of last night had him off kilter. His quest to find the diary had been as fruitless as finding listening devices, which cast doubts for him about Marilyn's credibility. Not for the first time. But the lack of lurking henchmen, the diary, and evidence of taps had lessened his belief of her being in danger. At least, apart from self-harm.

"Just recently." She cracked an egg. Pieces of shell followed into the bowl.

"You've been to the doctor, for a check-up, I mean?"

"No, not yet. But I know the signs." Marilyn smiled as she dug the shell out with a spoon. "I've been pregnant before, just not...successful-ly." She tightened the belt of her robe and raked her fingers through her hair.

Seeing how the admission pained her, Charles regretted his direct-ness. For years the press and tabloids had splashed her miscarriages and childless state across its pages.

"Who else knows?"

She rubbed the back of her neck, then let her head fall back.

Whether she was thinking about the question or growing uncomfortable with the conversation, Charles couldn't tell.

"A few."

"Does *he* know?"

Marilyn met his gaze and looked more serious than Charles had known her capable of.

"I don't know," she said.

On a hunch, Charles asked, "You told his brother?"

She hesitated but nodded.

Suddenly, Charles wondered if that explained her frantic behaviors: holing up in his office and making phone calls that afternoon. Had she been calling Bobby Kennedy, anxious for news of JFK's reaction to her pregnancy? If she had in fact spoken to Bobby, did she threaten him with a news conference, announcing the impending stork visit, if Bobby didn't tell his brother? Or had she promised to go public with the news if JFK didn't follow through on divorcing his wife?

But that was all speculation on Charles' part. He could easily picture the Kennedy men shunning Marilyn, avoiding her numerous calls, ignoring her threats, all in an attempt to discourage her, and to insulate JFK from further interactions with her.

Despite his frustrations with her, Charles felt an ache for Marilyn. She'd never get the acknowledgement she wanted from JFK. Regardless of an announcement or a child, the Kennedys would deny everything. And they'd blame her behavior, her *outrageous accusations*, on the drugs and alcohol. She made it too easy, especially with her behavior at the Madison Square Garden event.

Charles wanted to reach for her, touch her hand, the way he did when he gave clients a difficult diagnosis.

"Marilyn, you have to realize this baby...well, first and foremost, you should see your doctor right away. Make sure you're healthy. And you need to be careful in everything you do and with who you tell. For your sake, as well as the baby's."

"You're very attractive when you're concerned about me."

Charles ignored that.

"And you have to accept that...the baby's father may not choose to be with you. Are you prepared to handle this on your own? To keep the paternity a secret until it can be proven?" Charles couldn't believe what he was saying.

She closed her eyes, as if she were letting the avalanche of his words glide over her. Then she ran her hands up and down her arms, like she was chasing away a chill.

"I thought he loved me and wanted to be with me."

Charles believed her but wondered why Kennedy. Of all the men who'd been part of her love life through marriages, affairs, or short relationships, why had she become consumed by him? Was it simply because he was forbidden?

"Sometimes, it's not that easy, Marilyn."

"I thought I could finally be happy."

Charles avoided the obvious statements, those prickly reminders: *He's married, and he's President of the United States. He's not an actor changing spouses the way he changes roles.*

But he had no interest in defending the man.

He thought back to his conversation with Bert that night in his office. Bert told him Kennedy had no intention of dumping his pretty wife and shacking up with Marilyn. Was Marilyn refusing to believe it because Kennedy had made her promises? But according to Bert, there was no on-going affair and getaways for their trysts. He said Kennedy and Marilyn had only been alone together in Palm Springs and that Marilyn was *trying to turn it into something it ain't.* Marilyn had mentioned Palm Springs specifically, but when was that? Months ago? Long enough for Marilyn to discover she was pregnant, Charles presumed.

Bert said nothing about Marilyn being pregnant. Seemingly, that was the only point where his trove of information fell short. But he had mentioned Kennedy's *unsavory friends*, who might get rough with Marilyn if she kept talking about the affair.

Just then, Charles remembered the telephone call he'd intercepted last night. The caller had warned if Marilyn didn't pipe down...*they ain't gonna be nice about it.* A sentiment almost verbatim to what Bert told him.

Bert has an inside connection to this mess!

Charles' mind kept patchworking the pieces together. If Marilyn

had just told Bobby Kennedy about her pregnancy—during a telephone call from Charles' office—and the Kennedy men were just
learning the news, those threats against her were sure to escalate.

"Charlie?"

Marilyn's endearing voice broke him from the runaway trance of his
thoughts.

"Sorry." He sighed and shook his head, though it brought little
relief from the onslaught of revelations.

Charles knew what it was to be that man, lying or pacifying his
paramour to satisfy his desires. Not caring about her emotional fallout. But he also knew that Marilyn was capable of clinging to her
own fantasies. His biggest concern now was figuring out how to
help her.

For starters, he made the snap decision not to tell her about last
night's phone call. In his mind, relaying the threats would only
heighten her anxieties, and potentially stoke her irrational behavior to
increase. He couldn't say who the caller was anyway. And maybe he
wanted his own secret to keep from her.

"What do you plan to do?" he asked.

Marilyn's answer was suspended as the back door swung open and
Eunice joined their morning party.

"Oh, Dr. Campbell, it's good to see you again—and so soon." She
stopped short of wiggling her eyebrows at him it seemed, but a smirk
of approval brightened her face. "I'm so glad you're here." In a whisper,
she added, "I hate the idea of her alone, especially with those G-men
about." She patted him on the arm once again.

Charles had no response and didn't bother addressing her false
paranoid notion. Because he could've told her that he'd searched the
house and found no listening devices, but that would expose his
snooping and invasion of her privacy. Another secret he didn't mind
tucking away.

"I need to be going," he said.

"Must you?" Marilyn asked in that breathy voice of hers. She placed
her hand on his forearm. "We haven't enjoyed our breakfast yet."

"You're in good hands now." He glanced at Eunice and smiled; she
returned the gesture. "Perhaps I could call later and check on you."

Marilyn found a piece of scrap paper and scribbled her telephone number.

"Or you could just come back later," she said as she handed him the slip.

Maintaining his grin, Charles took the paper and avoided meeting Marilyn's gaze. He bid the ladies farewell as he retreated out the back door. A cowardly move, he thought, but he could live with that.

———

HE SPED through the empty streets of Brentwood, wishing it could relieve his mind. Marilyn had put him in a difficult position. If she were wrong about the baby, then he had neglected his duty, some might argue, in having her admitted and evaluated for psychiatric care. If she really was expecting and a child was born, well, he couldn't think of a bigger national emergency. Aside from Khrushchev launching Russian missiles at the U.S.

The consequences of both scenarios were lost on Marilyn.

On an impulse, he stopped by his office and picked up the reel-to-reel tape of Marilyn's session and the file Bill Stewart had given him on Marilyn. He couldn't rationalize it at the moment, but he intended to keep both items handy, in case a need arose to destroy them.

As he neared his home in Compton, visions of headlines and the fallout from a Kennedy-Monroe love child dissipated from his mind. Anticipation entwined his insides over the conflict that was sure to spark when he faced Helen.

He eased into the driveway, as if he could tip-toe the Buick across the asphalt. Since it was still early, perhaps he could sneak inside and pretend he'd arrived home in the middle of the night. Make it look as though he'd slept on the couch.

His plan fizzled when he saw Helen sitting there. Sharply dressed, though not in the Dior suit, she stood and stared at Charles a moment. Then she walked to the end of the couch and picked up a waiting suit-case. Nine years as her husband and over a dozen as a psychiatrist meant nothing, as Charles couldn't define the look on her face. No anger showed, just as no signs of tears lingered.

She strode to the front door and walked out without a word or even a glance over her shoulder at Charles.

There was no urge to go after her. No tug on whatever heartstrings he had left. Would there really be no confrontation? No altercation for Mrs. Winston or Mrs. Gibson to overhear? Although the calm was bound to be a temporary, Charles absorbed it, and with a grin, he welcomed the unexpected feeling of relief.

SEVEN

Charles appreciated the mindless distraction of watching Judith and Natalie taking turns, kicking a ball in the backyard. He had no idea how to tell them that their mother had left, or if she was even gone for good. Their reaction could be indifferent, like it had been for Charles, because when it came to Helen and her capers, it was impossible to know what it meant and if her absence would be permanent.

"My guess is that she's over in Culver City. Isn't that where she's doing the play?"

Charles left the sliding glass door and joined Pam at the kitchen table.

"That's what she said, but we never got into details about it." He took a swig from his coffee cup. "I just told her that I forbid it."

Pam hmphed. "It's no wonder she's gone. Are you going after her again?"

Soon after Charles was able to settle the shoplifting charges against Helen, she showed her appreciation by leaving him. For eight days he and the girls heard nothing from her. Charles kept the news hushed from the girls but had called Pam, checking to see if Helen had ended up in San Bernardino, but she never reached out to Pam. When he wasn't working and tending to the girls, he drove the streets of Los Angeles, looking for her. Just when Charles became convinced that he'd have to tell the girls the truth, that their mother had abandoned them, he found her sleeping on the back patio one morning. He didn't bother with many questions, and Helen offered no explanation.

To Pam's question, he shook his head.

"You know as well as I do that she's bound to sabotage herself."

Charles agreed. They both knew Helen had a passion for performing, but her talent and commitment didn't always match. Singing proved to be her stronger gifting but acting seemed to be her greater passion. She bristled, though, whenever she took classes and ended up quitting when her clash with the instructor affected her performance. Another reason he wanted to keep her from the play tryouts and the gig at the Peacock Lounge.

"There's nothing we can do." He sighed, then put his hand on top of Pam's. "Thanks for coming. You've always been there for me and the girls, and frankly, I don't know what I'd do without you."

Pam met Charles' gaze.

"She never appreciated you." She placed her other hand on his and caressed him with her fingertips, arousing Charles' goosebumps.

Had it been any other time in Charles' life, he would've lingered there, in her compliment and in that sympathetic look in her eyes. He would've leaned in and let his lips find hers and fulfilled his long-held desire for Pam. But he resisted. Acting on impulse had not served him well in the past, at least not long-term. Perhaps he had Marilyn to thank, for helping to strengthen his self-control. Was there a greater temptation on earth than Marilyn Monroe?

Besides, Charles had his girls to think of.

"I don't mean to put you in the middle of all this," he said, "but if you're sure they can stay with you for a while, it might be best for right now."

"Of course they can."

He slipped his hand away before he broke and told her everything. Never before had he fought so hard to bottle an array of emotions, from his worries about Marilyn to his anger at Helen for the antics she put him through. Helen could have at least put up an argument. He would have preferred a heated confrontation over the silent treatment. Over her walking out and leaving him with every responsibility. *You should be able to manage your family better*, Mr. Griffith's words echoed in his head, and he was right. Charles couldn't keep his family together. Even his father had succeeded, despite being an alcoholic. But Charles had to hush the raging thoughts. He refused to burden Pam.

He went back to the sliding glass door and watched the girls play.

Pam stood. "Take all the time you need. There's no rush. Come and get them when you're ready."

He crossed his arms as he stood there, pretending to focus while feeling mired in uncertainty.

———

AFTER PAM LEFT with the girls, it didn't take long for the stillness and emptiness of the house to rattle Charles. Although he and Pam said little about Helen—"Since Mommy is going to be away for a while working on her play, we thought you'd enjoy staying with your cousins." —he knew their suspicions would grow and questions would come. Shame poured over him, because it was easier for him to send them away than to face their tears. Or watch Judith's anxiousness manifest in her behaviors and Natalie pick at her food.

To fight the hovering depression, he tidied the house, more to have something to do than because of messes. He also brought in the tape recorder and reel of Marilyn's session from the trunk of his car and shoved them under the bed in the spare room.

He sat on the edge of the bed, the weight of a sleepless night pronouncing on him hard. For a second, maybe as a result of the lack of sleep, he considered going back to Marilyn's house. After all, shouldn't he see to it that she followed up with her doctor—her general practitioner and not Greenson—after yesterday's episode? Because Marilyn probably wouldn't go on her own, and she might not even tell Eunice that she had passed out by the pool.

Second thoughts had also crept in about the middle of the night telephone call he answered. The words, *If you ain't careful, they ain't gonna be nice,* chilled him. And that accent. Charles wouldn't swear to it, but if he had to guess, the guy sounded like he was from New Jersey. Not that it mattered, but the man had said, *...I never thought we gave things a fair shot between us.* Was he someone Marilyn had dated? Charles didn't like the thought, especially since the man was delivering a threat on someone else's behalf.

With that, he made up his mind. Marilyn deserved to know that— baby or no baby—someone was out to silence her, and he would promise to do his best to help her and to protect her.

AFTER CHARLES DOWNED MORE COFFEE, then showered and changed, he felt clear-headed. Coming off a sleepless night, he needed all the help and clarity he could muster. When he finished the top button on his shirt, he heard an odd noise coming from his backyard. The sound of running water.

Stepping out onto the patio to investigate, Charles was dumfounded at the discovery of Bill Stewart.

"Afternoon there, Dr. Campbell." Bill, a cigarette between two fingers, waved a hand. With his other hand he aimed the nozzle on the garden hose, spraying water onto a flower bed. "I thought your azaleas could use a drink. Looks like they're dying, and no wonder, it's been a hot one this year." A pensive smile appeared.

"What are you doing here, Mr. Stewart?"

"Funny you should ask that, doc, because I was gonna ask you the same thing."

"Excuse me?"

Bill looked over the backyard and nodded. "Nice home you got here."

Charles shifted his weight, racked his mind for something useful to say. Nothing came.

Bill eyed Charles. "She sure seems to like you. I guess I could see why. But you should know, she toys with people, especially the fellas. Men fall for her, all the time. It's like she's got some power." He shook his head. "But when she gets bored, forget it."

"Mr. Stew—"

"Tell me if I'm wrong, but didn't we—the studio—hire you to help Miss Monroe. From what I've seen so far, nothing much has changed."

"Well, it's only been a few days. You can't expect—"

"Let me tell you what I expect—what the studio expects." He twisted the brass nozzle, shutting off the water, then tossed the hose aside. "We need her in working condition. That means I need her to focus, to be able to show up on set every day. You see, we're thinking about bringing her back to finish the picture. Seems her co-star, Dean Martin, decided he won't film without her. That puts us in a bind because Marilyn isn't the easiest actress to work with." He walked over to Charles and stood a few feet from him. "And I don't need her head cluttered with notions about a romance, or any other fella-of-the-moment." He looked Charles over from head to toe.

Charles picked his words carefully.

"Mr. Stewart, I don't usually discuss my clients with others."

Bill chuckled. "We're not dealing with *usually* here." He enjoyed a draw on his cigarette through a thick smile. "I'll be direct. A little champagne in your office. Spending the night at her house, doing a little grocery shopping for her—hey, that was a nice touch, doc—but that ain't what we had in mind when we picked you for this job."

Blood pulsed to Charles' face.

"You might be helping yourself to some hanky-panky," Bill said, "but it's only gonna confuse her more. The best thing you can do is put her on something and get her straightened out. No more of this flapping her gums telling anyone who'll listen about her rumored love affair with Kennedy. Bottom line, doc, we want her under control and keeping her mouth shut."

Charles suspected the rumor about the baby hadn't reached him or the studio yet.

"Look, doc, I understand this broad is a lot to handle, like juggling fireballs. But trust me, it's in your best interest to finish the job, if you know what I'm saying." Bill dropped his cigarette to the patio and snuffed out the spark with his foot. Then he headed toward the gate and lifted the latch.

Before leaving, he turned to Charles.

"And, uh, heard about your wife. It's a shame, her leaving you. She sure is a looker."

BEFORE BILL HAD SET foot on the sidewalk out front, Charles telephoned Pam and made sure she and the girls had arrived safely at her house. Hearing Pam's voice, and that calm, steady tone of hers took the edge off Charles' anxiety, but he still feared they'd been followed. He spoke to the girls briefly and promised them he'd see them soon.

Thanks to Bill's impromptu visit, and his clear message that every aspect of Charles' life was being watched, he felt trapped. Suffocated.

When he'd agreed to take on Marilyn as a client, perhaps he'd been arrogant and too ambitious. He sincerely believed that he'd been hired to help her. To save her from her demons and addictions. That he was the lone man for the job.

Now, he was certain Bill Stewart had set out to make Charles a puppet. The man didn't care about Marilyn's health and well-being any more than Greenson did, as far as Charles was concerned. Like Marilyn had said, *they think they own you*, and looking out for the bottom line was a studio's top priority.

Putting Marilyn aside, Charles couldn't shake his unease knowing his privacy, and possibly his safety, had been compromised. How had Bill gathered such intimate details? Known about Helen's leaving, which had only happened that morning? Charles wanted to break out of his own skin.

He packed a small suitcase, then retrieved the money he'd stashed in the shoe box. Inwardly, he marveled that Helen hadn't found it, but the instant his fingers touched it, the money Bill had paid him nearly a week ago for Marilyn's sessions, repulsion charged through him. He put the money back inside the shoe box, then abandoned it, much like he did his house.

THERE WAS ONLY one place Charles could go now, and strangely, it was the last place he belonged. But since he knew his professional relationship with Marilyn was over—though it never qualified as professional—he told himself his actions made sense as he zigzagged his way back to Brentwood. Of course, he kept any eye out for anyone who might be following him, namely Bill Stewart. Constantly checking his mirrors and searching for any signs of a trace, he suddenly understood true paranoia.

Fleetingly, he wondered how many other patients, besides Marilyn, that he had fallen short with. Although Marilyn's behavior proved distracting, he had allowed it. *Failed psychiatrist* could be added to his list of inadequacies. However, the thought didn't nag him as he might expect, not with other matters weighing on him.

A developing revelation shifted him from the self-induced doldrums. *Marilyn isn't crazy or delusional, she's only trying to protect herself!* Many people saw her as nothing more than a dumb blonde, especially men, and she played into that. But perhaps she'd gone too far with the persona, making it difficult for people to believe her otherwise. And to soothe her disappointments, she turned to medications and alcohol, unaware of the cumulative damage.

If that were the case—that Marilyn had been truthful all along— then he had to consider that her claims about a baby were real, and that it wasn't just a ploy to get back at Kennedy for using her then snubbing her.

A crazy plan struck Charles. He'd convince Marilyn to run away with him, to leave Hollywood behind. When he thought about it, she had few attachments. The film studios considered her a risky commodity. Her house lacked warmth and personal touches, suggesting she didn't feel rooted and at home. The people seemingly closest to her, including Greenson and Eunice, had done her little favors in the way of truly looking out for her and taking care of her.

Most important of all, he reasoned, he'd claim the baby was his own. Yes, he'd be a father to that baby. He'd take care of Marilyn and her situation in every way. They'd both start over, stronger and smarter from the mistakes they each had made. Charles saw it so clearly. This was his chance to redeem himself as a man, and to make up for his failings as a father.

The more Charles churned it through his mind, the more it made sense. They would pack and leave today. Under the circumstances, a speedy departure was a must. He'd get the girls from Pam's, and they'd venture off for good. Where they ended up didn't matter. The details would iron out as they went along.

Suddenly, he laughed out loud.

"Yes, Helen, the day you left me, I ran away with Marilyn Monroe!"

Charles couldn't recall the last time his heart had felt so free and light, even if was only to last for a few moments.

WHEN HE PULLED up to the abode on Helena Drive, Charles was hit by a tidal wave of hesitation, and confusion. Two cars and three vans were parked in the driveway. Charles thought there had to be a mistake, or that he'd mistaken the true location of Marilyn's home.

But then fear paralyzed him. What if he was too late and the warning from last night's caller wasn't heeded soon enough? Or had Marilyn lied about dumping the medications and now suffered from an overdose?

Slowly, his anxieties evaporated as he watched the activity that flowed from the house. No emergency vehicles were present. Or reporters. A fair sign that things were normal. At least normal for Marilyn.

On his way to the front door, Charles passed two people who buzzed by him and headed for their vehicles, paying little attention to him. Once he stepped inside, Eunice greeted him merrily.

"I've come at a bad time?" Charles asked Eunice, after he freed himself from her quick embrace.

"Of course not! Marilyn's in her room, getting ready." Eunice prattled back toward Marilyn's bedroom and waved for Charles to follow.

"What's the occasion?"

"Tonight's the fundraiser for the Children's Fund, an organization that helps orphaned children here in Los Angeles. Everyone in Hollywood will be there! Marilyn loves this type of event." With the palm of her hand, Eunice gently pushed the door open to Marilyn's bedroom.

The sight of Marilyn staggered Charles. Although several people surrounded her, tending to her hair and tailoring her dress, Charles focused only on her. Sheathed in a pure-white gown, she radiated like a spotlight. Her womanly curves, highlighted and enhanced by the dress, made Charles feel as if he had wet sponges for knees.

What kind of man had he been, spending the night with her and not exploring the canvas of her body? Acting as though he had a sacred vow of chastity to protect and uphold.

I'm such a fool!

Marilyn turned and noticed Charles.

"Oh, Charlie, you're here!"

He realized he'd been slack-jawed and staring.

"Sorry to walk in on all the commotion. I just thought I'd stop by and see how you were." He feared he sounded pathetic.

"I'm glad." She gave him a smile that made his body temperature rise and a dabble of perspiration threaten.

"Looks like you're in for a grand evening." Charles knew he was groping for words.

Marilyn's face lit up. "You should come with me!"

"Oh, no, I couldn't."

"She could use an escort!" Eunice added.

"Well, I couldn't—I can't."

Marilyn escaped from her primping entourage and stepped close to Charles.

"Please, Charlie, it would mean so much to me!" Her hand rested on his chest.

"Don't you already have a date?"

"No." Marilyn sounded hurt, and her playful expression cracked into a pout. "I don't have anybody."

Charles bowed his head and lowered his voice so only Marilyn could hear.

"I'm not right for this. There must be someone else you'd prefer who's...better suited for this than me."

"Please don't make me go alone." Her voice broke, and Charles detected tears in her eyes. Was it the ploy of a good actress, or the raw emotion of a needy woman? Either way, Charles knew it didn't matter. Why bother holding out against her charms and sweet pleading?

He sighed. "Even if I could go, I don't have the right attire."

"Oh, Billy is here." Marilyn swept herself over to Billy Travilla and slid her arm across the top of his shoulders. "Why, he's the best designer in L.A. He can fit you up with something in a jiffy. Right, Billy?" Billy simply nodded. "Then it's all set!"

"Marilyn—"

"You're in good hands with Billy. He's a perfect genius with clothes!" She resumed her place among her attendants while Billy ushered a politely protesting Charles into the spare bedroom, and Eunice clapped with delight.

CHARLES COULDN'T DETERMINE how long it took, but when he emerged from the room, donned in a tuxedo, he had to admit, whatever reservations he had about going and not being adequate enough to mix among Hollywood's darlings, left him.

He scanned his appearance in the floor-length mirror, provided by Billy and his at-your-door services. Aside from healthier pocketbooks, Kirk Douglas and Cary Grant would have nothing on him. And with Marilyn on his arm, he knew he'd be the envy of every man.

At the same time, he hated this. Being ambushed, once again, by the demands of Marilyn the star, and giving in as though he had no backbone. But what was the alternative? Acting as her escort for the evening kept him by her side and meant she would be protected.

"It's time, Charlie!" Marilyn said as she emerged from the room.

The sight of her entranced him. Never had he seen a more beautiful woman. Her confidence matched the vivacity of her sparkling dress. Every inch of her exuded that glamourous sex appeal that defined her both on screen and off.

She reached out and took Charles by the hand.

With Eunice at their heels, wishing them a good time, like an adoring mother watching her daughter leave for a school dance,

Charles and Marilyn, hand-in-hand, made their way outside to the waiting car and driver. Charles' disgruntlement softened at the sight of the white Rolls Royce Phantom. The driver opened the door. Charles and Marilyn slid into the roomy, tan-colored interior. So did two other men. One joined him and Marilyn in the back, challenging the roominess, while the other sat up front, next to the driver. Marilyn didn't offer an explanation and wasn't disturbed by their accompaniment.

As they made their way to the Roosevelt Hotel, the man seated in the back with them, whom Charles hadn't been introduced to, talked with Marilyn in an endless stream, outlining the details of the night's event. Who Marilyn would sit with and at which table. Who she would be photographed with, and so forth. The man riding up front, also nameless to Charles, peppered in remarks, leaving no room for Charles to chat with his date. More annoying was the fact that Marilyn was oblivious to Charles' irritation.

She didn't even notice my suit!

His brilliant plan of running off into eternity with Marilyn seemed absurd now. As much as Charles despised playing the dupe, he was getting his fair share of practice at it.

When the car screeched to a halt alongside the curb, Charles' door was opened for him. He stepped out to a red carpet at his feet, flanked by red-velvet ropes and throngs of cheering, waving people on both sides. His eyes drifted over the sea of smiling, jubilant faces, and his feet felt rooted to the ground. A nudge came from behind as Marilyn appeared from the car and took her place by his side. Her reaction nearly matched the crowd's enthusiasm. She greeted them with her electric smile and waves in every direction.

Behind his forced grin, Charles feared Bill Stewart, or some lackey of his, had to be in that crowd watching him.

Charles went along, gently prodded and pulled by Marilyn as she led him by the arm. With the world watching, it seemed, he worked at playing and perfecting that role of *sucker* every step of the way.

AFTER THEY EASED down the red carpet, pausing for pictures and chatting with reporters, they stepped inside the hotel, and she left him. Not that Charles was surprised. Listening to Marilyn-handler-number-one in the car, he had an idea of what to expect. Handler number two showed Charles to the bar, and instructed him to wait there.

Fine by Charles.

He bypassed the tower of champagne glasses and gave a *no thanks* shake of his head when a waiter held out a tray of filled champagne flutes for him to help himself to. A sharp focus for the night was best, he decided. Ginger ale became his new companion as he watched the Hollywood elite mingle.

"Waiter!"

Charles turned and found Sophia Lauren holding out an empty glass for him to take.

"I need another," came her deeply accented voice. She wasn't looking at Charles when she spoke. Her outstretched arm and hold on the glass appeared lax, as if she were about to drop it.

If he had to guess, Charles would surmise that she'd had her fill. Instead of correcting the Italian actress that he wasn't on staff, he slipped the glass from her hand, then placed it on the bar top and tapped for the bartender. When he had the bartender's attention, he looked to Sophia and said, "He'll get you taken care of, ma'am," and walked away.

That was precisely what Charles hated about movie stars. They all thought they owned the world and everyone in it. Most people in their lives served one of two purposes, either to worship them or serve them. Such arrogance bred self-destructiveness, in varying degrees, from his experience. And those had been the exact traits Charles wanted to snuff out in Helen, and to save Marilyn from. Actors thought they were gods and goddesses merely because they graced the silver screen. But considering the crowd outside and their reaction to Marilyn, Charles had to admit, maybe there was some truth to that. Even his own behaviors around Marilyn fed into the very notions he despised.

Before Sophia or any other goddess put demands on him, Charles ducked into the main ballroom. A mish-mash of faces filled the space. Charles swore he saw Rita Hayworth, Katherine Hepburn, and Robert Mitchum, as well as several former clients. But there was no sign of Marilyn or the handlers.

Charles went in search of the ladies' room.

After checking two different locations on opposite sides of the ballroom, he came up empty. He decided to search other areas. Quieter spots away from the commotion. As effervescent as Marilyn could be, she also struggled with being the center of attention. When that aspect of her personality flared, she would confine herself to her dressing room during filming. A tidbit Charles had noted from Marilyn's file.

As he walked the hallways of the hotel, the crowds thinned. On accident, Charles found the kitchen. Waiters, real waiters, bussed in and out of the double-hinged door carrying trays and pushing carts. Charles changed direction and thought he was about to end up in a boiler room or laundry area when he spotted a group of men.

Half a dozen in number, they were situated just out of the light and around the corner of a corridor. Smoke haloed them, and their at-ease postures suggested that they weren't part of the kitchen staff, as did their attire. Tuxedo jackets were fitted onto the backs of folding chairs. One man occupied a chair, legs apart and arms resting on his legs, his head hung slightly. Another man leaned against a wall, braced by his shoulder, with a smoking cigarette nipped between his fingers. Others stood. One paced leisurely.

Charles eased against the wall, listening to a sudden instinct to remain unseen. Although Marilyn wasn't among the men, Charles edged closer. He had no business with them, didn't know them, but a sudden curiosity lured him closer. He came upon an alcove where a rack of white coats hung. Charles presumed they were uniforms for the kitchen staff. Stealthily, he slipped in behind the garments and moved to the edge of the nook. Cautiously, he peered around the corner and saw he was five or six feet from the men. Since none of them had detected him or noticed his movements, Charles breathed easier. But he knew a sound or sudden movement would give him away since he was now close enough to eavesdrop.

"Look, there ain't nothin' to worry about," said the man pacing.

"Knock it off, Frankie," said a man who was standing. "You can't downplay this anymore."

"Everything is under control," Frankie replied.

"We've had too many close calls," said the standing man.

"Yeah, but the press is keepin' mum. That's the important thing." Frankie kept up his leisurely pacing and stepped into the patch of light. When he turned around, Charles felt his eyes go wide as he recognized the man.

"And I told her the fling was over," Frankie continued, "to stop calling."

"It's not good enough," said another man. "She's a loose cannon. You know she's bound to talk to somebody. Somebody we can't contain in time."

Silence beat until the seated man lifted up his head and asked, "What about the diary?"

Frankie looked to a man who hadn't spoken. The man, who had been slouched against the wall, straightened, and as he did so, the light glimpsed his face. As did Charles.

Bill Stewart!

"Still workin' on it," Bill said. "We got someone on the inside, keepin' an eye out. It'll turn up."

"Look, Bobs, stop worryin' yourself over this." Frankie gave Bobs, the seated man, a good-natured slap on the back. "I'll take her out to the lodge in a week or two. If anything needs...taken care of...we'll do it then."

"The last time I talked to her," Bobs said, "she sounded crazy. All she did was go on and on about the two of them getting married, how he'd promised her. And she said she was going to do something drastic if he kept ignoring her and refusing to take her calls."

"Yeah." Frankie glanced up at a man behind Bobs. "I called her the other night and set her straight. You gotta give her a minute. Let it sink in."

"She called my office three times last week," Bobs said. "Even when I told her it was over, she didn't seem discouraged. This can't go on."

"Maybe if you tell her in person?" Frankie asked. "Here. Tonight."

Bobs took his time before nodding slowly, and added, "But I can't be seen with her."

Charles had heard enough. He moved from his vantage point and eased out of his hiding place. He had to find Marilyn, fast, and get the hell out of there.

EIGHT

Turmoil racked Charles. Was this what it felt like to be on the verge of a nervous breakdown? Pressed and challenged from every side and heightened by anxiety? No, he had to retain his ability to focus and stick to reason. Despite the fact he'd just overheard a famous singer and a band of goons collude with the attorney general over a troublesome actress.

There was a chance he was wrong. None of the men said her name. Or made a specific reference to her affair with the president. But they *had* mentioned the diary, and Charles recognized *Frankie* and Bill Stewart without question. Although the seated man kept his back to him, Charles was convinced it was Bobby Kennedy. *Bobs*. Distinguishing that East coast accent was second nature for Charles. And with all the television, newspaper, and magazine coverage, who couldn't identify a Kennedy from any angle? Maybe he wouldn't swear to it, but he was certain.

I've got to stay level-headed.

Several things troubled Charles. For one, Bill Stewart had mentioned *someone on the inside*. Was that *someone* watching Marilyn? The person she believed was in her house? And was there another someone keeping tabs on Charles? In a strange way, it made sense, since Bill Stewart knew every move and misstep he'd made in the last week.

Then there was Frankie. Frank Sinatra to his fans. Without a doubt, Charles knew Sinatra had been last night's caller. Mention of the lodge and telling her the affair was over echoed what the caller had said. And Charles had been right about the New Jersey accent.

He wanted to find Marilyn and whisk her out of the hotel before Sinatra and his men had a chance to find her and set her up for a private meeting with Bobs. He didn't trust a single one of them. Even at a public event with gaggles of reporters and a high risk of them being seen together. Because it seemed to Charles that men like the Kennedys and Sinatra got away with everything. He feared what they would do to Marilyn if they caught her alone.

Not having carte blanche access throughout the hotel magnified his disadvantage. Along with the fact he didn't have a band of thugs at his side. And what if he bumped into Bill Stewart?

Charles ignored his worries and searched for Marilyn.

Applause sounded from the ballroom at times. Charles knew there was a chance that Marilyn was in there, seated and enjoying the evening, and possibly wondering what had become of her date. If she wasn't in her seat, had anyone noticed? Charles wondered if the handlers were looking for her as well. Had Frank Sinatra and Bobby Kennedy up-ended the night's agenda?

Despite walking the corridors and poking his head into various unlocked rooms, Charles came up with nothing. He checked several floors. There was also no sign of Sinatra or Kennedy or Bill.

Charles decided to check the stairwell. Almost immediately, he heard soft cries. He scrambled toward the sound and found Marilyn, on the floor and huddled in a corner.

"Marilyn, are you all right?" He bent down and took her into his arms. At first, she hardly noticed and kept crying. He held her, hoping she felt a sense of security in his embrace. "Did they hurt you?"

"No," she whispered.

"Let's get you out of here." Charles helped her up.

She dabbed her eyes with the back of her hand, but the puffiness and redness remained. The sight of the smudged make-up on her hand seemed to reignite her awareness. "I can't be seen like this."

"Don't worry. We'll head straight for a cab," Charles said. "Ready?"

Marilyn calmed herself, nodded.

With Marilyn's hand in his, Charles led them to one of the building's side exits. Once they were outside, he popped open the door of a waiting cab. They ducked into the backseat and pulled away from the curb. Charles looked back and felt relieved that no one came running out after them.

He breathed easier and sank into the seat. Glancing down, he noticed he and Marilyn were still holding hands. Intent on imprinting the image into his mind, he stared at their fingers, laced together with skin touching skin. Could the two of them belong together? Build a life?

When he looked up at her profile and saw the make-up smeared around her eyes, he reached in his pocket for the handkerchief. Carefully, because he didn't want their hands to untwine. She thanked him when he handed it to her and used both hands to wipe away the cosmetics. Charles ignored the letdown that came when she slipped her hand from his.

An urgency struck him. He needed to tell her what he'd overheard and who he'd seen. More than ever, he had to convince her to leave Hollywood. He feared her life—the baby's life—depended on it.

When he looked at Marilyn, though, his eagerness faltered. She stared out the window but appeared not to focus on anything. Her shimmer had abandoned her. Listlessness engulfed her. The dress, which had been perfect hours before, seemed too tight and unflattering now.

"Marilyn, what happened back there?"

For a moment, she sat in silence.

"It's not fair."

More silence followed. Charles said nothing, only waited for her. He squeezed her hand, hoping it might comfort her.

"All men care about is control," she said. "They don't know how to handle a woman who speaks her mind and knows what she wants. They want us all to behave like trained poodles. Well, I've had enough!" She faced him. Suddenly resolute. "I want to be in control of my life."

He thought he understood. For much of her career, Marilyn had been typecast in dumb-blonde roles, and her fame had skyrocketed. But she'd also been vocal about wanting to play more challenging characters. Contract obligations had often made choices for her.

After marrying Arthur Miller, she again mentioned the hope of being taken more seriously in her films, as if her union with a famous writer gave her talent more credibility. But her dramatic turn in *The Misfits*, with the screenplay by Miller, sparked little interest in fans and moviegoers. Not long after, Marilyn endured her third divorce.

When Charles considered her history with men, from her very first husband, James Dougherty, when she was a teenager to her affair with JFK, and every man in between, was it any wonder she was crying? But he wanted to know what had happened to her at the Roosevelt. Did Sinatra and Bobby Kennedy manage to get to her, and if so, what had they said? Charles hesitated though, asking her point-blank, because he worried it would upset her again.

"You need to be careful, Marilyn. Now isn't the time to do anything crazy."

"But that's the problem, isn't it? Everyone thinks I *am* crazy, because of my mother and her ailments."

From what Charles knew, the mother was still tucked away in an asylum in Los Angeles. Research had shown a correlation between mental disorders and family members, that such disorders could be hereditary. He didn't know the full details of Gladys Baker's medical history or diagnosis, but he was sure that it didn't match Marilyn's struggles. Not perfectly.

Although he hadn't spent a lot of time in productive sessions with Marilyn, he would tentatively classify her condition as Hysterical Neuroses. She experienced feelings of apprehension with no obvious cause, fears severe enough to prevent an individual from routine activities, and irrational anxiety attacks. It explained why she was often difficult to work with, and when such fears were combined with reckless doses of pills and alcohol, there was no controlling or predicting the resulting behavior.

The treatment for Hysterical Neuroses included behavior therapy, psychotherapy, and drugs. None of which, Charles believed, would cure Marilyn. Not now. He saw her best recourse as abstaining from prescriptions. Medicine had done nothing for her.

Whether Greenson or any of Marilyn's other doctors would agree, Charles didn't care.

"Your mother and all she's been through, that's not you, Marilyn." He believed that with proper care and lifestyle changes, Marilyn could overcome the shadows of her past and a grim future. But she would have to want it more than he wanted it for her.

She smiled at him, as though a weight had been lifted.

"I've been thinking," Charles said carefully. "Perhaps you should consider taking an extended vacation. You've been under a great deal of stress lately, and some time away might do you good."

"Oh, I don't know, Charlie. I got a phone call this morning after you left. The studio is reinstating me on the picture. I wanted to tell you tonight, so we could celebrate." She flashed an impish grin with a return of playful glimmer in her eyes. "I can't really go away now."

Charles had to cap his anger. How could she be blind to her own hypocrisy? Wasn't that maneuver simply meant to control her, the very thing she just raged against? Why else would she suddenly be reinstated when none of her issues had been resolved?

"Then forget a vacation. Just come away with me. Permanently."

He couldn't say he was proud of his flimsy proposal—or that it truly qualified as a proposal—but he'd done it. He'd invited Marilyn Monroe to run off with him.

She gasped. And for a moment, Charles was suspended between apprehension and glee. Apprehensive that she could accuse him of being crazy, slap him even; gleeful that she might accept, and kiss him fully.

"Charlie," she said in that breathy whisper, "oh, you're such a wonderful man."

She cupped his cheek in her palm and held his gaze.

"I want to show you something." She turned her attention to the cab driver and gave him an address.

The area didn't ring with familiarity for Charles. He'd go along, let her have control, even though the change in destination didn't provide the hint of an answer for his proposition.

WHEN THE CAB stopped in front of the Actor's Studio, Charles couldn't deny the piercing disenchantment he felt. Why had he expected, hoped for, a spot with romantic potential? Before he became needled with too much disappointment, he recognized his own double standard. It was fine for him to criticize how every man had treated her or shackled her with expectations while he struggled with vexation over not taking advantage of her vulnerability last night and sleeping with her. Questioning his manhood yet pretending he was the Lone Ranger of chivalry.

He paid the cabbie, and they approached the building. Dwelling on his imperfections dissipated.

The Actor's Studio was a well-known training ground for students and hopefuls who aspired to hone their craft and work their way from struggling wannabe to box office darling.

"This is like a second home to me," Marilyn said.

Charles took it in as he noted the affection in her voice. However, the likes of Marilyn Monroe sashaying up to the front door didn't match up to the structure's dilapidated appearance. A former warehouse, if Charles correctly recalled, that had not seen renovations. At least from the outside. Some of the windows were cracked. Rust served as the primary embellishment, and the signage was faded. Classic markers of humble beginnings, though Charles wondered if that was the intent.

"Good memories, I assume?"

She nodded. "I wouldn't be who I am today without Lee and Paula."

The Strasbergs, famous for their devotion to method acting, were familiar to Charles, and he knew they had taken Marilyn under their wings. Lee spoke fondly of Marilyn to the press, going so far as to say that she was one of the greatest talents he'd ever worked with, second only to Marlon Brando. In the last several years, Paula (*that wacky acting coach*, as Bill Stewart referred to her), accompanied Marilyn daily, when she was on set, because Marilyn claimed she couldn't work without Paula by her side.

"Looks like it's closed."

"I know the secret to getting in." Marilyn winked and indicated for him to follow. She went around the side of the building and retrieved a key from a hidden crevice that Charles didn't have a chance to notice. Seconds later, they were inside.

"It's nothing like the studio in New York," she said. "That building is as small as it is old. It was a church in the 1800s, but in some ways, I guess it still is. A sanctuary for actors." She laughed at her cleverness.

"What are we doing here, Marilyn?" The edge in Charles' voice carried through the empty auditorium.

"Did you ever want to be an actor, Charlie?"

"No."

He stayed put while Marilyn seemed to know her way in the dark. Moments later the crank of a lever sounded, and lights illuminated a stage. Charles realized he and Marilyn were standing in the wings, where thick curtains shrouded them from the vacant audience. Marilyn walked to the center, where a circular beam of spotlight awaited.

"I thought it would be so easy." The haze and pure whiteness of the light gave her an angelic glow. "Always pretending to be somebody else, especially since I had so much trouble being me. Nobody wanted to be me, and nobody wanted me, growing up." A somberness tinged her words and wasn't lost on Charles. "But in front of the camera, I could do anything. I could transform my whole world." With her arms outstretched and her head tossed back, she whirled in circles and spun until her feet tripped her up. She fell square on her derrière.

Charles made no move to help her and went with the assumption she didn't want her performance interrupted.

Staying on her bum, she put her palms flat on the pinewood floor and faced the empty seats of the auditorium.

"They always told me how much they liked me," she said with a breathy satisfaction. "Producers, directors. And people would come up to me all the time and tell me they loved my pictures." Her chin dipped and her voice lost its delight. "But hardly anyone said I was talented. Not until I met Lee and Paula. But now, I don't know if I believe them anymore."

Charles took his time moving closer to her but was careful to stay out of the light.

"You don't have to live with it anymore, Marilyn. The critics or the pressure. You can leave everything. Hollywood, the studio, Greenson, the—" *Those damn Kennedys!* He couldn't say it, not without sounding like a jealous chump. But who was he kidding? She probably lost every ounce of respect she had for him back in the cab when he acted like a lovesick fool. Assuming she respected him at all.

He gritted his teeth. The only means he had left to keep from airing his irritation. She wanted control and freedom, but she didn't want to make the tough choices necessary to change her life. Even if there was no hope of her leaving Hollywood, she couldn't have it both ways—playing the vulnerable, helpless damsel yet wanting to be taken seriously as an actor when she couldn't show up on time or stick to a regular schedule.

Marilyn got up, seemingly unmoved by Charles' words. "Lee and Paula, they've always been good to me and tried to help me. I don't know why, but sometimes, standing in front of the camera terrifies me. My confidence runs away, and it doesn't seem to matter how many movies I make. I can't hold on to it. The only thing that's made a difference is Paula. She comes and helps me with my lines, and when the fear balloons up, she knows how to talk me through it. I know it's awful, to need her so. And Lee, he's been so patient with me, too. You know I've shared everything with them, about my mother and my past. Lee taught me how to compartmentalize my feelings, how to put them in a box in my head and pull them out when I need them for a scene." She turned to Charles' gray silhouette, flashed her shimmering smile and stood straighter. "He once told me I was one of the best actresses he'd ever worked with. *Me!* Norma Jeane, who never knew her father and never had a real home."

Charles understood how the damage from her childhood was deep and possibly irreversible. He'd seen it before, even in other actors. There was no medicine that cured the ache of abandonment, but the numbing stupor of drugs and alcohol proved swift and reliable. Marilyn was similar. When her emotional scars flared, from her broken marriages, lost babies, or fizzled affairs, those were the times when she sank inside herself. And the curtain came down.

Charles wondered if her encounter with *Frankie* and *Bobs* back at the Roosevelt Hotel had triggered a downward spiral for her.

"I know about Sinatra and the others," Charles said. "I overheard them tonight, talking about you."

Wonderment lit up her face.

"Did they hurt you? Threaten you?"

"No, Charlie. It may not seem like it to you, but they care about me," she shrugged and brought out that coy grin, "in their own way."

"You're wrong, Marilyn." Charles kept his clenched fists as his sides, determined not to touch her. "They only want to make sure you stay quiet. To control you—can't you see that? Think of what they would do if you exposed your affair with Kennedy. And once news breaks about the baby, they'll do anything to protect Kennedy—even if that means committing you to an asylum."

He hated mentioning the asylum but was desperate to make her understand and share his urgency. As he expected, the threat of being institutionalized gave her pause.

"Come with me." He surrendered to his desire to touch her and took her hand. There was more he wanted to say. Promises and declarations swelled in him, tempted his tongue, but he couldn't let them escape. He knew that trusting an infatuation would lead down a road of peril. Still, he wanted her. Wanted to tear his life apart, if that's what it took to rescue her and save her from ever being used again. Even if she didn't love him.

Marilyn glanced at their hands together, then at Charles. With her other hand she threaded her fingers into the back of his hair and pulled him into her. She kissed him fully. Charles responded with a passionate restraint, afraid of what would happen if he lost all control.

Then, she released him and sighed.

"Oh, Charlie," she said, her breath mingled with his, "don't you see? I can't go now. Why, that's the last thing I should do! I've got to show them, Charlie! Prove to them what I can do. I'm going to fulfill my contract, and then I'm only going to work for Marilyn Monroe Productions. I'll fight for the best scripts and make the films I want to star in. Maybe I'll play Joan of Arc! No matter what, I'm going to show them that they can't chase me off."

Charles wanted to argue and to tell her about the phone call from Frank, that her paranoia was justified, and that an *inside man* was intent on finding her diary. But he recognized that fiery determination in a woman. Once it rooted and cemented its hold, there was no shifting her from her decision. Helen had proven that.

"You don't need me for that." It was one of the most selfish remarks he'd ever made. He knew it was wrong, not reveling with her in her newfound clarity and optimism, as any good psychiatrist would. Hadn't that been his goal, only days ago, to help equip her to take care of herself and waylay reports about her out-of-control addictions? The zeal he'd had for the cause drained away. He could no longer deny the obvious—he wasn't meant to be the man who saved her. Burdened with defeat, he stepped back from the edge of her spotlight and turned toward the exit.

Marilyn said nothing as he shoved the door open, but he felt her eyes on him, and worse, he sensed her disappointment in him.

NINE

He took a cab, alone this time, to his office. Drunk on rejection, he slumped inside and up the stairs. The only thing worse, Charles imagined, would be returning home. Once inside, he fought the urge to telephone and check on the girls. Pam would know something was wrong, and he couldn't explain it. What good would he be to his girls now anyway?

The fact that it was Sunday evening thwarted his plans to swing by the liquor store and purchase a bottle of whiskey. Perhaps it was best. But a new inspiration struck. Charles retrieved the champagne bottle Marilyn had brought in for her impromptu and belated birthday celebration that he had placed in the refrigerator of the lounge. Modestly chilled but flat, it would do.

In full-pity mode, it didn't take him long to finish off the bubbly. He grew dizzy, nauseous. Alcohol never treated him well, and he knew better than to torture his body. In his deepening haze, Charles relived the sparse, confusing moments he'd shared with Marilyn in that office. The way she breathed life into the room the day she first visited. The internal conflict he felt, having Marilyn and Helen in the same room. Marilyn's head in his lap.

He collapsed onto the couch, ran his hands along the burnt-orange-colored fabric as he closed his eyes and pretended he could feel her there still.

Dreaming of his Marilyn, forgetting that he was angry with her, and accepting that she didn't—couldn't—love him, he faded into a drunken sleep.

THE SMELL of smoke combined with the intense heat from the flames and startled Charles awake. He sprang to his feet, realizing his office was on fire.

With his hand covering his mouth and smoke stinging his eyes, he stumbled his way down the stairwell, through falling debris, and out to the street below. Charles distanced himself from the building, then took in the scene while panting in fresh air. Black smoke billowed from the deteriorating roof. Firefighters arrived. Bystanders gathered in the still-dark night. Charles felt disoriented and couldn't help wondering if he'd done something to trigger the blaze. His head throbbed and only fuzzy recollections reeled through his mind. Had he caused this?

Wrestling with the uncertainty, Charles thought it best to get out of there. He was still wearing the tuxedo, a feature that was sure to draw him unwanted attention in the middle of the night. He'd never be able to cover the distance to his house on foot. His only recourse was to get to a payphone and call the one person he could trust in a crisis.

WHEN BERT DIDN'T ANSWER, the panic in Charles spiked. He had to get off the streets and avoid being seen. Keeping to the shadows, he made his way to Bert's apartment. Disheveled and covered in a coat of perspiration, his nerves began to settle when he reached Bert's. Cautiously, he leaned in close and rapped his knuckles on the door. He thought he heard noises within and hoped he wouldn't have to knock again to fully wake Bert.

"Chuck, is that you?"

Adrenaline jolted through him as Charles turned and saw Bert approaching from behind.

Once he was closer, Bert took in Charles' appearance. "Do I wanna know what's going on here?"

"I'm not even sure what's happening." Charles breathed easier and wished he could clear his head. He was curious as to why Bert wasn't fast asleep at this hour but let it go, being in no position to ask questions.

"What are you doing standing out here? You know where the key is." Bert glimpsed the doormat.

"Yeah, but I thought I should knock before I barged in on you in the middle of the night. You probably sleep with your gun under your pillow."

Bert chuckled and unlocked the door. "Can't be too careful in this town."

Charles sighed a breath of relief when he stepped inside. As he shed the tuxedo jacket, aches struck him. Not-so-gentle reminders of sleeping on the office couch, however short his slumber had been. A mild headache thumped, but otherwise, he concluded he'd escaped a raging fire unharmed.

"Looks like you had quite a night." Bert cocked his head, eyed Charles. "Can't say I ever pegged you as the type of guy out all night roaming the streets in a tuxedo. Already got the Feds chasing you down?"

Charles wouldn't bother mentioning his date gone wrong with Marilyn. "No, nothing like that. Just a fluke. An accident. My office caught on fire tonight—while I was inside."

Bert flashed a wide-eyed expression. "That sounds pretty serious. You sayin' someone's tryin' to kill you?"

Such a thought hadn't crossed Charles' mind. "Kill me? What made you jump to that conclusion?"

Bert raised his eyebrows, as if the idea needed no explanation.

"Oh, come on. You're sounding paranoid."

"You and me both work with different kinds of paranoid, Chuck."

Charles considered that. He had been paranoid that night he stayed at Marilyn's. Had even searched the place for listening devices.

Then he'd driven back to Marilyn's home, glancing in his rearview mirror repeatedly and taking a longer route in case he was being tailed. Perhaps he couldn't completely dismiss the notion. But someone out to kill him...and make it look like an accident? It seemed a far stretch, and no one knew he would be at his office. Then again, Bill Stewart had confronted him with personal insights that nobody apart from him and his family should have known.

"It's preposterous." He said it more to himself than Bert.

"Is it? Weren't we just talking about national security a couple days ago?"

"Yes, that had little to do with me."

"Chuck, I don't think you realize the full scope of what's going on here. We're not just talking about a guy making it with a blonde babe. We're talking about the President of the United States having an affair with the world's most popular actress, while there's a threat of nuclear war breathing down the country's neck. And some of the boys surrounding the president, trust me, they'll do whatever it takes to protect the guy—and I don't just mean from a death threat. I mean they'll protect him from looking bad in the public eye when it comes to this actress. Like I told you, Kennedy's connected with some, let's say, criminal element."

Maybe Charles was truly starting to lose his mind, but the mention of criminal element took him right back to the Roosevelt Hotel where he eavesdropped on Sinatra and Bobby Kennedy—and Bill Stewart. Hearing their conversation had frightened him enough to get Marilyn out of there. Terrified him of what they might to do to her.

Plus, it wasn't exactly a secret that Sinatra mingled with known members of the mafia. For all Charles knew, those other men present at the hotel—the goons—could've been part of that...network. As a fellow New Jersey native, Charles knew such connections, such *friends*, came in handy, especially for a celebrity who wanted to keep his hands clean.

And Charles wondered, if Sinatra really intended to make a play for Marilyn and pursue their relationship, did he wanted to send a message of *stay away* to the man frequently popping up in her life?

"I'm hardly a threat."

Bert raised his brows. "You wanna tell that to them?"

They ain't gonna be nice echoed in Charles' head. His thoughts spun to Marilyn. If someone had really tried to kill him in a fiery blaze, what had happened to her after he left the studio? He'd been a fool to abandon her.

Charles stood. "I need to check on Marilyn and see that she's safe."

"Whoa!" Bert stepped in front of him. "Slow down. You don't wanna do that."

"She could be in danger—or worse!"

"What are you gonna do? Run over there and tell her people are out to get her? Kill her? You think she can hear something like that? No way. I bet she gets spooked—and worked up more than you can handle. Think about it, Chuck! You need to lay low, get your head on straight before you go traipsing off."

Charles ran his hands over his face, as though it might calm his raging thoughts. Bert was right. Charles needed to think things through. He didn't want to endanger Marilyn further—or risk her having a psychotic break. He scarfed a breath and tried to craft a solution to helping Marilyn.

"What if you went over there?"

Bert paused. "To Marilyn's place?"

Charles nodded. "It's your specialty. Spying. I just need to know that she's okay."

Bert seemed to ponder the idea. "Yeah, I get it. I could go over, maybe pose as the gas man checking for a reported leak or something. See who's around, get a sense of things."

Charles balked. "I just realized, I left my car at Marilyn's house."

"You were with her last night?"

Charles worried he was giving away more than he wanted. "Long story."

Bert narrowed his gaze. "I guess you're in this deeper than I thought."

"We'll talk about it later."

"Come to think of it, how's Helen takin' all this?"

"She and the girls are out of town, visiting relatives in Sacramento." The ease of the lie surprised him.

"Oh. That's probably good." Bert told Charles to help himself to the fridge while he got him some clothes to change into. Then he grabbed his keys and put on his fedora. "Why don't you wait here. It's early so I can't go knocking on any doors just yet. Sit tight. This may take a while. I'll be back as soon as I can."

Charles wasn't thrilled with the notion but lacked a better idea. He watched Bert hustle out the door and hated that all he could now was pray that Marilyn was safe.

AFTER BERT LEFT, Charles showered and changed. Although he was glad to be out of the formal attire and refreshed, an unsettling came over him. He didn't like being in Bert's apartment with him gone, but he also had an itch to do something besides wait.

He dialed Marilyn's home telephone number. Hearing her voice would soothe his concerns. He'd apologize for last night, for leaving her at the studio, and not escorting her home like a gentleman. She had every right to be angry with him and chide him. Or maybe he would speak to Eunice and possibly gain insight into Marilyn's current situation. But no one answered, which only made him worry that she didn't end up at home last night.

His fears mounting, he flipped through the telephone book he came across in a kitchen drawer. When he found Dr. Ralph Greenson's office number, Charles dialed. His heart raced. What could he say in a matter of seconds to convey his concerns over a patient they shared? He quickly decided to declare it was an emergency, that he needed to find and speak with Marilyn. If that didn't work, he'd fib about Marilyn's poolside collapse and tell the good doctor she had attempted suicide and was a danger to herself. It was a stupid risk but the best he could think of under the pressure. A dozen rings later, though, it didn't matter since no one picked up.

Apparently, Greenson doesn't do early Monday mornings.

Charles refused to sit and stew in a stuffy apartment that unsettled him. He had an idea. A place he could check where Marilyn *should* be. He left a note for Bert on the kitchen countertop, simply stating that he'd return. Then, Charles slipped from the apartment, armed with new hope and full-tilt anxiety.

————————

AFTER GETTING LOST and losing track of the number of buses he took to get there, Charles arrived at Twentieth Century Fox's studio lot. At first, he blended in with a group of tourists and kept an eye out for signage for *Something's Got to Give*. If Marilyn wasn't home, Charles reasoned that she had reported back to the set having been reinstated on the film. Following through with her commitment to *show them* she was well and capable of finishing the picture. Exerting more control, in her mind.

As the group moved on, he lingered behind and took several dresses from a rack sitting outside a door. Charles flung the garments over his shoulder and searched for anyone who looked like a director or an assistant. He found a young woman with a clipboard, her attention focused on her writing.

"Excuse me, ma'am," Charles said. "I'm delivering these to Marilyn Monroe." He gestured to the dresses. "Wardrobe for her film. Can you tell me where she might be, please?"

"That film has been suspended." She barely lifted her eyes from the clipboard.

"Miss Monroe has recently been called back to work on the project. I was told to get these to her. Pronto. Do you know someone else I could ask?"

She glared at him.

"I just told you, filming's been suspended, but if you want to check at the executives' offices," she pointed with her pencil to the front of the building, "they're located across the lot, *far* from where I'm standing."

Charles took the hint that her patience with him had reached its limit.

"Thank you," he said as she walked past him.

With steady strides he made it to the Executive Suites building. He planned to ask for Bill Stewart's office. Perhaps turn the tables and put pressure on him for a change. Charles was greeted by a friendly receptionist.

"Good morning," he replied. "I was wondering if you could direct me to Bill Stewart's office, please." The receptionist, with distinct pleasure in her voice, directed him to the third floor, and Charles thanked her. His need for the dresses gone, Charles laid them on a chair next to the elevator.

Charles found Bill Stewart's nameplate beside the door to his office and entered after a quick knock. He couldn't wait to see the look on Bill's face and how he liked being ambushed.

But sitting behind the mahogany desk was a portly gentleman, probably nearing his sixties, wearing glasses, sporting a head of white hair—and was clearly not Bill Stewart.

"Pardon me," Charles said. "I'm looking for Bill Stewart."

"You've found him," the man said, tossing his glasses onto the desktop, "and if you're here to sell me the greatest screenplay of all time—"

"No, nothing like that." Charles had to think fast. "Is there another—"

The man ran his hand over his forehead. "If this is some kind of practical joke...."

His voice trailed off as a sudden realization hit Charles. *Bill Stewart wasn't with the studio, was he? That's why he showed up in my backyard and knew my every move. That's why I saw him with Sinatra and the others. He's with them; he's one of them!*

"Sorry to disturb you, sir."

With that, Charles retreated and hightailed it off studio property before someone decided to call the police.

WHY HAD he been so stupid? Charles cursed under his breath. He should have known Bill Stewart was a phony when he showed up in his backyard. Maybe before then—such as when he dropped an envelope of ten thousand dollars cash on Charles' desktop. Or maybe even the day he walked into Charles' office and played evasive with the need for him to help a troubled actress. But Hollywood didn't always operate above board, making it easy for Charles to believe at every turn that Bill Stewart was a studio executive, just doing his job.

Outside the gates of Twentieth Century Fox, Charles ducked into a cab and decided to head to Marilyn's house, despite the risks. Since he didn't know how Marilyn's evening ended last night, there was no telling who could be at her place. Running into Bert, once he got there, was also a possibility. If Bert had followed through with his plan to pose as a gas man investigating a leak, Charles didn't want to blow his cover.

When he reached Marilyn's, the driveway was empty. Even his car was gone. After several raps on the door and ringing the doorbell, no movement or sounded. Charles turned on the stoop, about to make his way to the back of the house where the patio doors would allow him a peek inside. But when he saw a white-haired lady across the street staring at him and clutching her white-haired poodle, he thought better of it. Attempting to save face, he smiled and waved to her. The woman's stoic expression didn't flinch.

Since the cab was gone, Charles started walking. He hoofed it, especially once he was out of the sightline of the nosy neighbor. Luckily for him, a gas station sat a mile away.

As he'd done earlier, he telephoned for a cab from a payphone. Flushed with discouragement and perspiring, he instructed the driver to take him to Oscar's.

Going back to Bert's apartment was probably a more logical destination, but Charles was still disturbed that his office building had been destroyed by a fire only hours ago. With Oscar's bar in close proximity to the charred remains, Charles hoped to glean some information from the locals.

He slipped in and sat near the end of the bar. Charles ordered a sandwich and an iced tea from the young bartender, who Charles wasn't very familiar with.

"By the way, do you happen to know what all the commotion was about down the street?" Charles aimed to sound casual.

"A building caught fire in the middle of the night. Looks like it could be arson."

"Sounds pretty serious." He hid his astonishment. "Do the police have any suspects yet?"

The young man shrugged. "Not sure, but someone saw a guy running away shortly after the fire started. And get this, he was wearing a tuxedo. Only in Hollywood, right?"

Charles nodded as the news sank in. Arson! And the police had a witness who could put him at the scene. Possibly. A lengthy investigation would unfold, he figured, and in that process, the police would question the building's occupants. How much of a description did the authorities have of the man in the tuxedo?

"Heard you been lookin' for me."

Charles looked over at the man sliding onto the stool beside him. Bill Stewart. At least the man he'd known as Bill Stewart.

"I figured it was time we meet, square up," the man said.

The bartender returned and asked the man what he wanted.

"Scotch."

"Who are you?" Charles asked when they were alone. He hated the cliché—confronting the stranger and dropping a basic question he likely wouldn't answer. Not honestly anyway.

"You think that matters now?" The man smirked, then shook his head. "I'm disappointed in you, doc. Thought you were the easy-going but skittish type. We gave you a simple job. All you had to do was stick to the task at hand. But I know she's trouble. Greenson couldn't handle her either, not the way we wanted. But then the next thing I know, you're showing up at the Roosevelt with her like a gentleman caller." He leaned in. "You shouldn't have gotten involved, doc."

"Marilyn was never really the problem. All this time, the press tried to make her out to be crazy, drunk, and erratic. But the truth is, she finally got tired of being used by men and the studio. She was trying to keep it together." *And escape their control!*

"That could be true, but what good is the truth, doc? People don't want truth. It ends up being too painful. Messy. But I'll give you some truth. A friend of yours suggested we use you, said you'd work out swell." The man shook his head again. "But I had my doubts. I'm not one to trust your kind. But this friend, he insists, says he'll keep an eye on you, that you two grew up together and he knows how to pull your strings. He'll make sure you get the diary."

Bert! A shudder jolted Charles. He'd been played, just as he suspected.

As for the diary, he could've told the man that Marilyn made it up and it didn't exist, but at this point, that might have been the only information he had over the guy. Leverage. Not that it meant anything or would do him any good.

"But it didn't work out that way," the man continued. "It's over, doc. No more playtime with the blonde. And just to be sure," he reached into his pants pocket, then slid an item, under his hand, across the bar top to Charles. "I took special measures to make sure you understand where I'm coming from."

A book of matches. Not just any matches. They were stamped with The Blue Velvet Room script and logo. The gentleman's club that served as Bert's preferred hangout. Charles took the matches and flipped open the top. On the inside flap, the address of his building was scribbled. One match was missing.

Shock washed over Charles. He couldn't speak.

"See what I mean about truth?" The man leaned in. "You ever try to see Marilyn again, and the police are going to be able to come up with a sketch identical to your mug. You catch my drift, doc?'

Charles could only stare at the matches.

"Bartender," the man said as he stood, "put my drink on my friend's tab. He's the one who really needs it."

TEN

Charles felt trapped in an episode of the Twilight Zone. There was no other way he could think to describe it. In fact, he could hardly think at all. Learning that his oldest friend had been part of set up struck a blow. Try as he might, though, Charles couldn't fathom why Bert had deliberately manipulated him into a scheme aimed at drugging and controlling Marilyn. Why get Charles entangled with mobsters—if that's what Bill Stewart *really* was—and practically offer him up as a sacrifice to Stewart, Sinatra, and the like?

Anger and disgust boiled inside him as he took a cab home. If anyone was there, waiting to take him out and finish the job, he'd face them head on because he was done cowering.

When he pulled up to his house, bafflement replaced his rage, seeing his car parked in the driveway. His best assumption was that Marilyn had it delivered from her home. Had Marilyn also been told that she wasn't to see Charles anymore? Was this her way of confirming that their association, their *relationship* was over? Having found no trace of her this morning, he feared the worst.

Numbness took over as he made his way inside. He envisioned crawling into bed for days and pretending the last week had never happened.

But Helen waited for him in the living room.

"What are you doing here?" Before she could answer, anger shot through him. He stormed over to her and grabbed her by the shoulders. "Have you done something to the girls? Have you hurt them?"

"No!" She winced from his forceful grasp. "I came to help you!" Fear glazed over her eyes, and she trembled in his grip.

Charles paused, having never seen her distressed and intrigued by what she meant.

"What are you talking about?" He let her go.

"They're going to kill you!" Helen said. "Your car, they cut the brake lines...they wanted to make it look like an accident—"

"You're part of this? This whole set up? This betrayal?"

Helen said nothing. Tears fell and she didn't look at her husband.

"Why me?" Charles asked.

She shook her head, as if she couldn't find the words she needed.

"Didn't I tell you these people don't like loose ends?"

Charles and Helen snapped their attention towards Bert's voice as he walked into their living room—pointing a Beretta handgun at them.

"All you had to do was keep her doped up, Chuck. That's the way they like her, doped up and pretty." Bert glanced at Helen. "Otherwise, dames ain't never worth the trouble."

"So you set me up." Charles clenched his fists at his side. Gun or no gun, he wanted to take a swing at his old pal.

"No, *we* set you up." Bert nodded toward Helen.

Charles glared at his wife and waited for her to deny it.

"I wanted out," she said somberly. "I wanted out of this house, and you out of my life. I don't belong here, with you, Charles. I never did. And last night, when you came to Bert's apartment...I was there."

The noises Charles heard from inside, before Bert surprised him from behind. Was that why he felt unsettled, being in Bert's apartment? Helen had been there, hiding.

Charles caught her side glance at Bert and the subtle smirk that tweaked Bert's face. Knots wrenched Charles' stomach.

"How long?" He barely managed over the lump in his throat. "How long have you been having an affair with Bert?"

"Ever since you had your own little side action," Bert said. "I told her all about you and your little tart. Then I promised I'd get her away from you someday. You never deserved her, Chuck, and she ain't meant to be no housewife."

"It's not supposed to be like this," Helen said, a whimper in her voice. "You can't shoot him, Bert."

"The only thing I care about is the diary." Bert forced his arm a little straighter.

Charles saw the anguish crest on Helen's face.

Silence beat, until Charles, recognizing the absurdity of the moment, felt an internal shift. The two people he loved most hurting him. One even planning to shoot him—for a diary that didn't seem to exist. Instead of intense fear, laughter bubbled up, and Charles couldn't hold it in.

"The fact I'm about to put a bullet in your head is comical?" Bert tightened his grip on the gun. "Where's the diary?"

"You went through all of this, used me, slept with my wife, and threw away a lifetime of friendship just to get Marilyn's diary?" Charles said between outbursts. His laughter petered out and Bert's expression morphed from anger to confusion. As Charles settled, Bert seemed to refocus. They became deadlocked in a piercing stare.

"It's in a heap of ashes," Charles said, "where my office used to be."

He took the matchbook from his pants pocket and tossed it at Bert; Bert snatched it midair and glanced at the cover. A knowing, satisfied smirk appeared on his face.

"For her sake," Bert swung his aim toward Helen. "You better be lying, Chuck."

"No, Bert! Don't do it!" Charles threw his hands up, as if that might hold Bert back.

Helen darted behind Charles.

Charles expected the gun to fire, but Bert didn't pull the trigger.

"Where is it!"

"Forget the diary! It's worthless," Charles said. "It doesn't mean anything, not compared to what Marilyn told me. She's pregnant with Kennedy's baby."

Helen gasped.

Bert paused, then, let out his own laugh.

"You expect me to buy that sack of goods? Maybe I ain't no hot-shot doctor like you, but I read that file they gave you. Miscarriages, abortions, and all that. Her insides gotta be so messed up that having a kid is impossible. You know what that sounds like to me? She scammed you, Chuck. If that's what she told you, then she reeled you in like a fresh catch."

Charles wondered, had Marilyn lied to him? Had it been a feeble attempt on her part to find that sense of control? Perhaps it was a means to distract Charles, as well. If he was concerned about a preg-nancy, then he might take greater care with prescriptions, lose focus on his main goal of subduing her, like Bert and the phony Bill Stewart had wanted.

"The diary, Chuck. Now."

"I told you, I don't have it."

"Then it looks like we're gonna have us a little accident here. Picture them headlines: *Respected psychiatrist to the stars goes crazy, kills wife then himself.* You'll finally be famous, Helen." Bert chuckled.

In that split-second Bert was distracted and lax in his own amuse-ment, Helen lunged at him. She and Bert tumbled to the floor. The gun fell from Bert's hand. Charles went for it. Helen thrashed, but Bert bucked her off him and rolled on top of the gun before Charles could grab it. Charles kicked Bert in the side. Bert crunched into a fetal posi-tion and felt for the gun. Helen landed on top of him. They twisted and struggled.

Until two shots were fired.

Charles stepped back, as neither of the two moved. Blood pooled on the floor. Then, Helen pushed herself off Bert and stood. She held the gun in her hand. Bert remained motionless. Charles knelt and checked for a pulse, but his old friend was dead.

"We have to call the police."

"No," Helen whispered. "I don't want to go to jail."

"This was self-defense. He was going to kill us both!"

"It won't matter. Do you know what would happen to my career? No," she shook her head, all the while focusing on Bert's face.

"Helen, you've committed a murder. We have to face this."

When their eyes finally met, Charles felt an abyss of distance between them. He knew instantly that he'd never convince her to own her share of the blame. Not in this situation or in the decay of their marriage. In their own ways they'd each tried to escape the mess they created, either by alienating the other or by ignoring each other's genuine needs in a relationship. Separation and distance weren't new to them, but the growing sense of its permanence was for Charles. He could live with that.

"Then go, Helen. It's what you do best." Charles said it without the snark she deserved. But now that it was over between them, he finally understood her, and he knew it was meaningless to judge her for her faults, for who she really was. There was no changing her. He should have realized it at the Diamond Club, years ago.

He was also now aware that Helen and Marilyn weren't that different. Just as he concluded that Marilyn would be better off sans pills and extreme measures, he realized that Helen wasn't a woman who responded to or changed because of pressures and demands. What would their life had been like if he had encouraged her instead of clinging to his predilections? It was too late to find out.

With a tear-streaked face, Helen stepped close and kissed him. Not a passionate kiss. A good-bye kiss, and for Charles, it was one of the most tender and most honest moments they'd ever shared.

"SO LET ME GET THIS STRAIGHT," LAPD Detective Stan Warnowski said, as he flipped back to the beginning of his notes on his spiral pad, "you killed this guy, Bertrand Miller, in self-defense. You knew him, met him at Berkley, and he was a client of yours."

"Yes," Charles said. "Several weeks ago he looked me up, and I was seeing him at my office, treating him for paranoid psychosis. Our sessions were troubling, though, as he believed in a variety of strange theories. He believed he was always being followed and that federal agents were hiding in his house. He even had hallucinations of Elvis skinny dipping in the community pool."

"No kidding?"

Charles nodded. "The other day he told me that fire keeps the hallucinations away. He grew hostile, even threatened to burn down my office, thinking that would cure him. And this morning, I found out my office building was destroyed, and the police suspect arson. Then he showed up at my home with a gun. Clearly, he was more disturbed than I realized."

"Mmm." Detective Warnowski pointed to a framed photograph on a side table. "This your family?"

"Yes, my wife and two daughters."

"And where are they?"

His nerves were frazzled. Lying intensified his turmoil but having a dead man on his living room floor worked in his favor. What kind of person wouldn't be shaken after someone—a client, no less—shot himself? "Thankfully they're visiting my wife's sister in San Bernardino."

"Lucky for them," Warnowski said. "No telling how this would've played out if they'd been here."

"Lucky, indeed," Charles said.

IN THE DAYS THAT FOLLOWED, Charles felt like a victim trapped in the aftermath of an earthquake, waiting for a rescue or a slow death. Much of the tale he fed Detective Warnowski was corroborated, thanks in part to Elliot, the janitor who worked at Charles' building. Elliot recalled seeing Bertrand Miller at Charles' office at an unusual hour and told Detective Warnowski, emphatically, that *something wasn't right with that man*. The book of matches had also been found in Bert's pocket, with the address of Charles' office on the inside flap.

When Detective Warnowski learned from Bert's landlord that Bert made a living as a shady private investigator, Charles knew that cemented Bert's character for the police officer. But interviewing Bert's landlord was a mere formality, after a tuxedo was found at Bert's apartment. The witness who had seen a man running from the scene of the fire claimed that Bert was in fact the man he saw that night.

A lack of evidence also worked in Charles' favor. The fire meant all his patient records, including those he kept on Bertrand Miller, were destroyed.

Baffling most of all for Charles was his ability to invent and sustain such lies. He bested Helen with the performance of his life, although he had no plans of duplicating the feat.

After getting the brake line in his car repaired, he visited Pam and the girls. Like Detective Warnowski, Pam accepted his narrative. He didn't like the mild deception, but he refused to implicate Pam by telling her what had really happened. However, he mentioned that he had been in touch with Helen, and based on their conversation, they'd likely never see Helen again. He choked up, genuinely, because his marriage was over and in the wake of everything that had happened, he hadn't had time to grieve.

Tears glistened in Pam's eyes. No doubt for her sister. Of course, Pam offered to keep the girls while the house was thoroughly cleaned and order restored.

Through the next couple weeks, Charles suffered a crick in his neck from looking over his shoulder, taking paranoia to a deeper level. At every turn he expected to find a gun in his face and someone new who'd been sent to finish the job of silencing him or demanding the diary. But there were also moments when Charles reasoned that Bert's death had bought him time. Because if Bill Stewart and gang really wanted him dead, now wasn't the time since the office fire and Bert's demise made the papers. Offing Dr. Campbell would be too risky, Charles hoped.

Late one evening, when Charles was relatively sure no one was following him, he went to Marilyn's. Cruising through the neighborhood, he checked for anyone who looked slightly suspicious. He even kept an eye out for the white-haired lady with the poodle. When his nerves were satisfied, and once he watched Eunice leave, he approached the front door and rang the doorbell.

Marilyn greeted him with a fierce embrace.

"Oh, I've been so worried about you." She released him and pulled him inside.

She offered to make coffee, which Charles accepted. Although he doubted her ability, because he assumed Eunice and others did such things for her, she handled the percolator better than cracking eggs. Charles resisted the urge to find her more endearing.

"I heard about the fire at your office," she said, as they sat at the kitchen table. "And that man trying to attack you in your home! I was worried that something might've happened to you, but the papers said no one was hurt."

Charles nodded. "Just the building." And Bert. He had no desire to elaborate on the truth about Bert. Like Pam, it was best to keep her in the dark.

She took his hand into hers. "I wish you would've come sooner. I...I didn't realize how much I enjoyed your company. You're so easy to be with, Charlie."

He was surprised that her touch had little effect on him, that his feelings for her had muted. Perhaps the incident with Bert and Helen had left him numb and incapable of emotions. Or was he merely in the process of reconciling from the hurt and betrayal, with no room left for other notions?

"What's a girl to do without someone to talk to? Someone she really trusts."

She flashed that innocent, wanton look. Charles thought of their kiss. Long and passionate as they stood in a halo of light at the Actor's Studio. Not that it led anywhere—or convinced her to run off with him. Now wasn't the time to dwell on fizzled fantasies. And if he were honest with himself, being with Marilyn reminded him of what a failure he'd been, professionally speaking. Their therapy sessions had gone nowhere, and if that had been Marilyn's intention all along, well, it was a moot point now. But it still irked him.

"The night of the fundraiser, after you left me at the studio, I thought you were angry with me and never wanted to see me again." She removed her hands from his. "I thought about going to your house again..."

Charles detected a thread of guilt in her voice. For a brief instant, satisfaction danced in his chest. He liked the idea of her being pained over him. But the feeling faded quickly.

"I shouldn't have left you alone that night. It was selfish of me, and I'll always regret it."

A softness came over her face, as if he'd said what she needed to hear. "You want to know something? I'm always going to wonder if I should have taken you up on that offer. Maybe that's exactly what I need, to leave L.A. and reinvent myself somewhere else. Become someone else."

He nodded. "A fresh start is a nice idea, but doing it, that's the hard part." Perhaps he couldn't resist, slipping into the psychiatrist role. Sincerity filled his remark, and he didn't harbor any anger that she couldn't walk away from her complicated life.

"I don't know why, but sometimes I'm afraid to do what's right for me, and I don't always know what the right thing is until it's too late."

If he were hearing her correctly, she was telling him that her instincts had often led her wrong. An ache rose for her because he didn't know the best advice to give.

"I hope you realize, Marilyn, that you're capable of making good decisions for yourself."

She smiled but turned her attention to the coffee pot.

"It doesn't matter now, but I was wondering," Charles said as she poured their cups, "who was it that decided you should see me?"

"You mean you don't know?"

Charles shook his head.

"Well, I'm sure you know my friend, Frank."

"Sinatra? Of course."

"Well, he wanted me to talk to someone." She placed the cups on the table, along with creamer and sugar. "He thought it should be someone new to me, and he told me his friend knew a friend. A doctor in Inglewood, who wasn't too uptight."

He smiled at her laugh. If he had to guess, the so-called Bill Stewart served as a go-between for Sinatra and Bert. Maybe Bert thought he'd get in the good graces of Old Blue Eyes and the Rat Pack, wiggle his way into the high life. At the same time, Bert could dismantle Charles' life. A life he'd probably been jealous of. The cherry on top for Bert would've been getting his hands on Marilyn's diary. He could've handed it off to Sinatra himself, and Sinatra would've used the diary to wiggle his way further into the Kennedy fold. Bert would've been a hero among con men. If all had gone right.

Naturally, Charles felt he couldn't ask Marilyn about the diary. Fabrication or not, it was private. Although the simple record of her musings had cost Charles a friend and almost gotten him killed, he couldn't justify crossing that line. If Marilyn was writing down secrets she'd gleaned from the Kennedy men, perhaps it was her talisman and safeguarded her from Sinatra's boys. One thing was certain, she'd hidden it well.

But there was a sensitive topic Charles believed he deserved the truth about.

"There was never a baby, was there, Marilyn?" His tone was mild, unaccusing.

"I thought there was." She shrugged and sat back in her chair. "Or maybe I just wanted there to be a baby. So he couldn't deny me."

Control, Charles thought.

"You were right," she said. "He never loved me. I'm not even sure if he's a good man anymore."

"Does this mean you're moving on, from the relationship I mean?"

"I don't care if I never speak to Johnny or Bobby again."

Charles gave a half-grin but was elated to hear her say it.

"Besides, I have better things to do than mope around for a man who doesn't want me. I'll be working again soon."

"Back to the film with Dean Martin."

She answered with a pressed-lip smile, then hesitated. "I've also been talking to Joe."

"Your ex-husband?" Charles couldn't hide his surprise.

She nodded. "After you left, and after everything that happened, I just needed to talk to someone. So I went to see Joe. He let me stay with him for a few days. It was nice. Maybe I shouldn't say this, but I could see us getting back together. No one has ever really loved me, not like Joe."

Considering Joe and Marilyn's past, Charles couldn't understand what would make her think that reuniting could work. Had Joe entered counseling for his abusive behavior or was she willing to live with his destructive temper? Marilyn was returning to acting and returning to filming the kind of scenes that had bothered Joe. What would be different?

Reminding her about the past and warning her about Joe was pointless. She didn't crave his advice. It was too late for Charles to play the role of psychiatrist.

Just as it was too late for him to mention the telephone call he intercepted from Sinatra. Too late to share that Sinatra had expressed a desire to rekindle their relationship. Sinatra would have to fend for himself.

Charles couldn't deny the glow that came over Marilyn when she mentioned Joe. Ripples of grief and hatred struck Charles, knowing he'd never be the man who made her light up like that. Maybe she wasn't as capable of making good decisions as Charles had thought.

"Promise me you'll take your time, Marilyn, that you won't make any sudden decisions. Being on your own for a while, without a serious relationship, might be good for you. Same as being away from the pills and alcohol."

The last part had slipped out. What did Charles truly know about her habits? Nothing, but he sensed the woman before him was clear-headed and sincere. This was their first normal conversation, absent of antics and propelled by honesty.

Marilyn giggled. "I'll have all weekend to think about it. I'm going to the lodge."

The lodge?

"Sinatra's place?" Charles asked, more ruffled than he intended.

"Yes," Marilyn said. Her enthusiasm waned. She tilted her head ran her fingers through her hair, as if his question made her uncomfortable.

The Cal-Neva Resort and Casino, often referred to as the lodge, was a hotel that straddled the California-Nevada borders on Lake Tahoe. Frank Sinatra had purchased the place a couple years back as a getaway for him and his famous friends. Joe Kennedy had been close pals with its former owner, and the Kennedy family was known to frequent the spot for its privacy. Sinatra had a helicopter landing pad installed for arrivals and departures. Charles even heard rumors that underground tunnels allowed Sinatra, or perhaps Kennedy, to move to different areas of the lodge unseen.

Charles couldn't help his reaction. He knew things Marilyn didn't.

Specifically, he thought of Frank's promises to Bobby that she'd be taken care of, out at the lodge. A sinking feeling inside Charles told him it was too late to admit everything he knew. Even if he told her the whole story, it would come across as contrived, mentioning it now.

He had to find solace in knowing she had let go of her obsession with Kennedy. Maybe a weekend at the lodge wasn't the worst idea. If Sinatra had feelings for her, surely, he cared about protecting her.

"I need you to promise me something else," Charles said. "Promise me you'll be careful, Marilyn, and that you'll follow through with what you said about taking care of yourself."

She laughed a little and seemed to like the suggestion.

"Anything for you, Charlie."

EPILOGUE

"That was the last time I saw her," Charles said to his grandson. He couldn't keep the tremble out of his voice. "A week and a half later, she was dead."

"So she was never really pregnant with Kennedy's baby?"

Charles attempted a shrug, but his hunched shoulders didn't help.

"I read the autopsy report, years later. There was no mention of a pregnancy. But I doubt there would be. Rumors also came about that an abortion was performed against her will at Sinatra's lodge that last weekend. But there were other rumors too." Charles couldn't go further. Gossip had swirled that once she was intoxicated and drugged, a sex tape had been made. Meant purely for blackmail and to be used against her if she didn't leave the Kennedys alone. "There's no telling what the truth might be."

His remark reminded him of what Bill Stewart had said: *Truth is painful. Messy.* If that were so, Charles could finish his days without knowing the truth about her last visit to the lodge.

"You think the Kennedys killed her, Grandpa? Or had the mob do it?"

Regret welled in Charles' chest. Had he said too much? Was he wrong to share his history with the boy?

"I gave up thinking about that years ago. Doesn't do any good. All I know is I should've made her listen to me. Should've made her leave with me. I didn't do my best to save her."

Charles knew it was possible she *had* committed suicide. Because if the rumors surrounding her visit to the lodge held an ounce of truth, he could picture her, desponded when she fully realized what they'd done to her. They also could've threatened to show Joe the tape, which would've destroyed any chance of their reconciliation. Combined, all those factors would've proven too much for Marilyn. Her depression could've prevailed.

According to newspaper reports, Eunice had been staying with her. When she noticed the light along the bottom of Marilyn's bedroom door around 3:30 am, she went to check on her but found the door locked. Repeated knocks and shouting didn't rouse her. Frantic, Eunice called Greenson, who broke into Marilyn's room through a window. He pronounced her dead. Authorities were called, and Greenson pointed out an empty bottle of sleeping pills that had been prescribed three days earlier by a doctor named Engelberg.

No diary was found.

"Grandpa, you couldn't have known what was going to happen."

"I suspected, but I was too selfish and too worried about myself, I suppose."

There had also been the sting to his pride with Marilyn turning down his proposal to leave L.A. for a new life.

"How did you hear that she'd died?"

"A radio announcement. I panicked. I made good on my decision to leave. I packed up your mother and her sister and headed back here to New Jersey and started over. Changed occupations. Then I met and married your grandmother six months later."

"Wait, whatever happened to Helen?"

"I lost track of her fairly quickly. From what I heard, the part in the play fell through, but she performed at the Peacock Lounge for a few weeks. She landed some small parts in movies. Movies you've never heard of though. A couple years later she died. Never made it big. After the gun fired and Bert was dead, she gave me a look that said I was never going to see her again. And I didn't."

Charles thought of Pam. They'd kept in touch after Charles moved and remarried, but maintaining a connection proved painful. His adoration for her never faltered, but after he married Lorraine, staying in touch felt disrespectful to his new wife. Last he had heard, Pam and her family were still in San Bernardino.

"But what about in court," his grandson broke in, "during the divorce? You saw Helen then."

Charles pressed his parched lips together.

"I never divorced Helen. Not legally."

The implication sank in, both for Charles and his grandson.

"Does grandma know?"

"She knows everything. There's no need to complicate this any further. Lorraine Campbell is and always will be your grandma." When he thought of Lorraine, an aching pride battled within Charles. She'd been easy to fall in love with. Judith and Natalie attached themselves to her effortlessly. Judith's nervous habits of biting her nails and chewing her blanket lost their hold. Natalie's bedwetting and picky eating subsided. They all found a fulfillment with one another. Lorraine's craving for love, the girls' want of a mother, Charles' need of mending a broken heart.

For reasons unknown, Charles and Lorraine never had children of their own, but there was never a doubt between them that they belonged together.

Although there were times Charles sensed a stirring in the girls, questions that brewed or wanted to form, they never surfaced. Perhaps they worried that if they dwelled on it and asked about Helen, she would return and replace Lorraine. Charles could only guess how their minds worked. He stayed ready, all those years, to face their concerns and to share the truth, but they didn't discuss Helen and her fate. That suited Charles, too.

There it was again: truth. Charles had distanced himself from his time with Marilyn, the collapse of his marriage, and Bert's death, convinced that burying such secrets was best. Safest. After all, he never freed himself from the dread or suspicion that Bill Stewart or one of his kind would appear, or that one morning Charles would start his car for the last time. That was life, he supposed, as a dangling loose end.

"You couldn't have saved her, Grandpa," the boy said.

"Who?" he asked, breaking from his thoughts.

"Marilyn. There was nothing you could've done."

Now, sitting on that bench, and for the first time since the summer of 1962, Charles wondered if his grandson was right. By the time Charles met her, what hope did he have of saving her, especially when he barely managed to save himself and his girls from a life of ruin.

Apart from Marilyn's careless behaviors, there were also those who wanted her silenced. Against such powers, he was hopeless.

No, Marilyn wasn't his. Like Helen, she'd stolen a piece of his heart and branded herself on his psyche. He made bedfellows with the decades-old blame and no longer remembered life without the burden. But today, surprisingly, he found a serenity by sharing his truth. Was it peace? A final freedom, perhaps, that would enable him to live and die at the same time.

He enjoyed a soft chuckle. Subtle enough that his grandson didn't notice, which he was grateful for. Because Charles needed time to figure out how he would tell his family today's news. The doctor confirmed what Charles already suspected—his cancer had spread, and at the most he had two months to live.

He dug in his pants pocket and removed his keychain. His fingers quaked but he found the little silver key and held it up.

"I want you to take this. Go to the Greyhound depot. Find the lockers. The number's on the key."

The boy took the key. "What's in there?"

"A recording. I don't know if it's any good, and you might have to find some ancient equipment to see if it still works. But it's one of my sessions with Marilyn. She told me...well, see if you can get it to work." The recorder had been tucked under the bed in the Campbells' spare bedroom the night Charles' office had burned down. When Charles made his hasty getaway back to New Jersey with the girls, he'd taken the recorder and tape reel with him, but he hadn't listened to it since the day after he recorded it. Reliving the details would be too painful for Charles.

"What do you want me to do with it?"

Charles considered that. "Nothing. I just want you to have it, and to know I'm telling the truth. Maybe there's no way to prove it's Marilyn Monroe on that tape, or even if there is, it doesn't matter. Not now. People have solidified their opinions of her and chosen the theories they like best. I couldn't destroy it. Just promise me you won't make a sensation of it, that you won't put it on the internet or create a spectacle. Marilyn…she's been through enough."

"I promise I'll take care of it."

"Good." He patted his grandson on the leg. "There's one other thing in the locker. Ten thousand dollars. It's the money Bill Stewart paid me for my sessions with Marilyn. Again, I didn't know what to do with it."

"But you and Grandma could use that—"

Charles held up a hand. "We've managed this long. We'll be fine. You keep it. Consider it an early inheritance, your only inheritance."

"Why are you telling me all this now, Grandpa?"

"It felt right."

The Kennedy empire had dissolved. Sinatra was dead. As was the golden age of Hollywood. Charles had outlasted them all. It wasn't a sign of his character or a mark of his integrity, and it made him no better than any of those men.

"You know how it is," Charles said, "when you first wake up from a dream? Good or bad, there are vivid fragments in your mind, and if you let it come, the story of that dream unfolds. In those rare moments when that happens, you can't catch your breath, and even though parts of it don't make sense, it all felt so real. But time is an enemy. Once you get up and get grounded in your world, the dream breaks up. Consciousness steals it away, and you wonder if you really dreamed it at all. That's how it was with Marilyn. A dream. A beautiful dream that breaks your heart."

AUTHOR'S NOTE & ACKNOWLEDGEMENTS

As with any work of fiction that meshes real people and real history with "what ifs", certain creative liberties have to be exercised in order to make the story work. One fabrication that is entirely mine is the invention of the Actor's Studio location in Los Angeles. Although the organization had been well established in New York since 1947, the West Coast venue wasn't open until 1968, and it didn't start out in a warehouse. I felt Marilyn's connection with Lee and Paula Strasberg was important enough that if the LA location had existed at the time, it would've been a special haven for her. Marilyn was devoted to her craft and relied heavily on their instruction, Paula in particular. Some fabrications are intentional and designed to keep the fiction aspect alive in the story, but on this specific point, I didn't want my research to seem slack or lazy. Thanks for understanding.

I'm fortunate when it comes to my writing that I have a fabulous network of support. Much thanks to my friends at Buckeye Crime Writers.

-MK

ABOUT THE AUTHOR

Mercedes King is an Ohio native with a degree in Criminology from Capital University. She is the author of the Jacqueline Bouvier Kennedy Onassis series, a four-book collection that offers a fictional peek inside the private life of one of America's most beloved first ladies. Harboring a love for mysteries, she also writes crime fiction. *A Dream Called Marilyn* (novella), *Grave Secrets*, and *Every Little Secret* are among her growing body of titles. She was also a proud short story contributor to *Columbus Noir*. An active member of Buckeye Crime Writers, she enjoys being part of the local writing community.

DEAR READERS

If you would like to join my mailing list for news and updates, get in touch with me at mercedeskingauthor@gmail.com . On social media, I'm most active on my Facebook page (here) and would love to have you follow along. If you have enjoyed my books, please share a 5-star rating and a short review on Amazon and / or Goodreads. Thank

Enjoy the following excerpt from *Jackie's Paris*, book 1 in the Jacqueline Bouvier Kennedy Onassis series.

JACKIE'S PARIS

CHAPTER ONE

Manhattan
April 1949

Poised and postured like the twenty-year-old debutante she was, Jacqueline Bouvier strolled into Schrafft's on the arm of her father. The scent of Sunday brunch—freshly griddled waffles and bacon—greeted them, along with curious stares from several female patrons. Jackie loved it, the charisma he exuded that effortlessly captured women's attention. There at his side, with sunlight streaming in behind them, she basked in the envy of every woman in the establishment.

As they followed the hostess to their table, her father's flirtatious glance seemingly waltzed through the restaurant, at least when he wasn't focused on the hostess's salacious saunter in her snug crème-colored skirt. Jackie took the seat her father held for her. The hostess promised that a waitress would be with them shortly, then departed with a tilt of her head and a subtle wink meant only for Jack Bouvier.

Was it any wonder? Jackie mused. Crowned with jet-black hair and sporting a thin moustache, he was often mistaken for Clark Gable. Dapper in every wool or tweed suit he wore, he never lacked for female companionship but showed no interest in settling down. His reputation as a womanizer, combined with his nutmeg skin tone, had earned him the nickname Black Jack.

"Pity that Lee couldn't join us." He draped the linen napkin across his lap.

Jackie grinned at him, attuned to his sarcasm. Friction often sparked between her sister and their father, which Jackie blamed on their parents' divorce. Lee's outbursts and penchant for drama tested and drained their father's patience. He never voiced his frustrations, but Jackie suspected he resented having to soothe and subdue her sister's cantankerous moods.

"She sends her love and regards," Jackie fibbed. Her request—insistence, really—on lunching alone with their father today had resulted with a bedroom door slammed in her face.

"Does she now? How thoughtful." Jack opened the menu and pretended to scan the selections he knew so well. For a man who had a varied and insatiable appetite for women, he remained faithful to the corned beef sandwich on pumpernickel, topped off with a shot of sour scotch. "And how is the rest of that brood, dare I ask?"

Brood was the best insult her father could hurl about the blended family of nine Jackie was part of. Quite comfortable in the lifestyle her stepfather's fortune afforded, she could tolerate her father's petty criticism and unveiled jealousy. An heir to the Standard Oil fortune, her stepfather practiced law, served in the government, and heralded a brokerage firm he'd established, while Jack Bouvier, a stockbroker himself, still hadn't recovered financially from the crash of 1929. When he wasn't gambling or bedding the mothers of Jackie's classmates, his alcoholism got the best of him. Nevertheless, nothing could diminish Jackie's adoration for her father.

"We manage." Jackie gave a feeble smile, careful not to injure her father's feelings. Her homelife held no interest for him, and she didn't want to risk putting him in a foul temperament. Not when she had such an important item to discuss.

The itch to change the subject took over. Jackie reached into her handbag and removed a folded pamphlet. Smoothing her gloved hands over the paper's crease, she did her best to flatten it before handing it to her father.

"What do we have here?"

"A fabulous opportunity." She sipped her water while he read the announcement, but her patience failed. "Smith College is offering a year-long student exchange program at the University of Paris, which would include classes at the Sorbonne. Vassar doesn't offer such a program, but I can still apply through Smith." Jackie pressed her lips together to stop her zeal from running away.

He skimmed the pamphlet, then shifted his gaze up to her.

"Paris?"

Jackie nodded.

"Are you certain this is a good idea, my love? I know you've had a taste of Europe, and Paris can be intoxicating. But living there—for a *year*—well, I'm afraid it would be frightfully expensive."

Jackie would be the first to admit that her seven-week holiday with family friends the previous summer had whetted her appetite for more of Europe. She dreamed of living there and being more than a passerby, but two things kept her from a life abroad—her parents and money.

"I realize that, Daddy, but I could board on campus instead of renting an apartment. That would save money, and I could find a job." Her enthusiasm waned with the last suggestion, though she hoped her father didn't notice.

Working held no appeal for her, not if it meant being shackled to a schedule and stuffed inside a dank building. She wanted to immerse herself in Paris, savor its art and architecture; but mostly, she relished the thought of exercising total freedom over her life—and escaping the tangible strife between her parents. If a job was required to secure her fantasy, then so be it.

Jack glanced over the paper again and set it aside. "Shouldn't you be enjoying everything Vassar has to offer a young woman of your age and standing?"

His real question wasn't lost on Jackie: *Shouldn't you be finding a husband?* Many women her age attended university as a glorified dating ritual and abandoned their studies once a proposal came along. Education and obtaining a degree were not secondary for Jackie. Though she was social, attending football games and weekend outings at Yale, her dating life had been fruitless. She often sensed her parents' growing impatience, but it wasn't her fault that she found most men dull.

"I have, Daddy, and that's the problem. Poughkeepsie is like a frumpy old spinster, who sips her gin and falls asleep in her housecoat." Jackie paused while her father enjoyed a chuckle. "There's nothing stimulating there, which is why I end up at your apartment."

Jack grinned, no doubt appreciating that his oldest daughter preferred retreating to his Manhattan apartment on weekends rather than romping on her stepfather's grand estate in Newport, Rhode Island.

"But now is your time, my dear. Why, you were Debutant of the Year. I would think that troves of worthless beaux would be salivating at your feet."

"All men are rats. Isn't that what you've been telling me for ages now?"

"No argument there." Jack withdrew his pack of Chesterfields from his pocket and lit into one.

"You see, this is the perfect time for me to go to Paris. I have no attachments, no one I'm particularly fond of, and just think, my French will become perfect while living there."

Their waitress appeared, and Jackie sensed a sigh of relief from her father, indicating he wasn't prepared to give his consent yet. He took advantage of the moment and exercised his charms with the young woman. In turn, she smiled and played coy.

As usual, Jackie mentally absorbed the exchange and envied the way he captivated women. She needed a dose of such magic since gentle persuasion was failing her.

The hesitance was because of the money, she knew. Her father wouldn't relent easily, even if his funds were abundant. Controlling the purse strings, as it were, of Jackie and Lee's lives was the only power—or influence—he still held over them. Although that was only in his mind. No trust fund would be forthcoming from their father. As it was, he barely kept up with their monthly allowance of fifty dollars each—a sum that paid for their cosmetics and little else.

But Jackie wouldn't let that pinch of resentment derail her determination. She deserved this trip, having fed her father's pride with her stellar academics and award-winning horsemanship. She gave him no grief, and her love for him never waned, even when rumors of his gambling debts circled or when he required another drying-out spell. Now, would be her father's turn to show his love and loyalty.

"I know it's a lot to ask, Daddy," she said once they were alone again. Employing new tactics, she rested her hands in her lap and tilted her head slightly, feigning resignation. "Perhaps I've acted too hastily. Maybe going away to study isn't ideal, but I'm aiming to make changes regardless."

Jack's gaze locked on hers. "Do tell."

"Like you said, living in Paris would be expensive, but that's true of life most anywhere. I was thinking of easing the burden on you and Mummy. I'm perfectly capable of reading and acquiring knowledge on my own, which is primarily what university life entails. I don't need Vassar, or the Sorbonne, for that."

"What are you getting at?" Jack squinted and tucked his cigarette into the corner of his mouth.

"Perhaps it's time I ventured out and started making my own money. I've been thinking about becoming a fashion model, here in New York. I could get an apartment—"

"Now, now, I'll not tolerate foolish conversation." He waved a hand in the air, as if to shoo away the suggestion. "You're a rare bird, my dear, and one of the things that makes you so extraordinary is your mind, that hunger you have for history, literature. You shouldn't abandon university just so you can make money. I won't hear of it."

"Then you'll let me go to Paris?" Hopefulness swelled in her chest. "It's only for a year, Daddy."

He reared back in his chair, his expression pensive.

"What does your mother say about this idea of yours?"

"I haven't told her yet." Jackie smiled. "I came to you first."

Jack beamed. The way he always did whenever Jackie demonstrated her devotion to him or gave him an advantage over Janet.

"Tell me, then, when you *do* mention this to your mother, what do you think she'll say?"

"I imagine she'll want to talk me out of it." Elation pulsed through her. Why hadn't she thought of using her mother's disapproval earlier?

He exhaled a puff of smoke slowly, and a Cheshire grin appeared from behind the cloud.

"In that case, my pet, we'd better make sure that all the arrangements are in place before you tell her."

To continue *Jackie's Paris*, click HERE.

BOOKS BY MERCEDES KING

The Jacqueline Bouvier Kennedy Onassis Collection

Jackie's Paris

Jackie's Camelot

Jackie's Greece

Jackie's New York

Historical Fiction Titles

A Dream Called Marilyn

Crime Fiction / Mysteries

Every Little Secret

Grave Secrets

Columbus Noir

Newsletter subscribers receive a FREE e-book for joining. Sign-up here.

Printed in Great Britain
by Amazon